Afraid Knot Copy

An Olivia Morgan Cruise Ship Mystery

Wendy Neugent

SWH Media, LLC

Niki:

Thank you for being a wonderful tía.

Visit
https://WendyNeugent.com/free-book
to get the e-book of Chico's Adoption
story for free!

Gotcha!

When Olivia walked into the pet store
to buy dog food for her mother's
chihuahua, she wasn't looking to adopt
a pet.
After all, traveling the world as an
entertainer on a cruise ship isn't exactly
pet friendly.
But she desperately wants to save the
bird from the nasty pet shop owner.
Not only is the pet shop owner mean to
the little parrot, but Olivia suspects that
he is up to no good.

Can she save the parrot and take down the pet store owner, or will the pet shop owner take Olivia out?

Get this mystery ebook for free and find out!

A shadow passed over Olivia, Hayley, and Rachel. Olivia shivered and shaded her eyes with her hand. She looked up to see what was blocking the sun.

"Tristan?" Olivia sat up, grabbed her coverup, and pulled it over her head.

Hayley flipped over, stretched, and grinned at Tristan. "Hey, there. You leading pool games?"

"I thought Nigel was doing pool games. Is he okay?" Rachel adjusted her towel and looked around the pool.

"Nigel is fine and yes, he is doing pool games. He should be here shortly." Tristan sat down on the end of Hayley's lounge chair and rested his hand on her tanned calf. "I have a situation and I was wondering if you ladies could help me out."

"Sure." Hayley pulled on her bikini strap, looked at her tanned skin and reached into her bag. She handed Tristan her sunblock. "Can you put this on my back?"

"My pleasure." Tristan squirted sunblock in his hand and slathered it on Hayley's back.

"What kind of help do you need?" Olivia asked.

"Did you all meet the Youth Counselor who was on the ship last week? Emerald?"

Hayley and Rachel shook their heads no.

"I met her." Olivia cleaned her sunglasses off with her coverup and slipped them back on. "She asked me to bring Chico by the Kid's Club last cruise so the kids could meet him."

A smile flicked across Tristan's face. "Really? I didn't know that."

Olivia frowned. "Is that alright? Should I have run it by you?"

"Oh, no! It is wonderful that you did that for the kids. How did it go?"

Olivia shrugged. "It went alright. There weren't a lot of kids onboard last week. The five or six children that were in the Kid's Club enjoyed meeting Chico. They said they'd never seen a parrot up close like that before."

"Lovely, did Chico enjoy the children?"

Olivia shrugged. "You know Chico, he loves attention."

"That's perfect. So glad it went well."

"Okay," Olivia cocked her head and squinted. "Glad you're happy."

Hayley swiveled towards Tristan. "Why all the questions about the kids' activities?"

Tristan shifted on the lounge chair and took a deep breath. "So, here's the situation. The parents' Meet and Greet was right after the lifeboat drill in the Kid's Club. I got contacted about a quarter past the hour that no one was in the Kid's Club with the parents. They were all waiting for a youth staff member to show up and no one did."

"You checked her cabin?"

"Of course. We contacted her roommate, Nell, and have put out a watch for her with security." Tristan shook his head. "This isn't like her. Emerald has worked for us on school breaks and over the summer for the past few seasons. She's very responsible."

Olivia's brows knit together. "Emerald is really nice. She even popped some unsalted popcorn for Chico in that popcorn maker they have for the kids when they play movies. She sent a bag home with us after we talked to the kids."

"That sounds like something she would do. She is good with the children and handles their parents, which isn't always the easiest task," Tristan swallowed.

“I’m quite concerned about her. She’s a lovely gal.”

“I’m sure they’ll find her soon.” Hayley squeezed Tristan’s hand.

Olivia leaned in. “Do you need us to help you look for her? We could start up here on Pool Deck and work our way down to B Deck. Do you know which deck her cabin is on?” She slid her feet into her sandals.

Tristan waved her off. “No, I don’t need help looking for her. Alex and his security team have that covered. They are checking the manifest to make sure she didn’t sign off early without telling me, too”

Olivia slouched. “Oh. Sounds like he has it handled, then.”

Hayley looked at Tristan through narrowed eyes. “What exactly does

Emerald going missing have to do with us, then?" She nodded towards Olivia and Rachel. "You said you need our help."

Tristan cleared his throat. "Here's the situation. We have families who are on board expecting the Kid's Club to be open for their children and we don't have anyone to staff it."

"That stinks." Hayley laid back down on her lounge chair.

"Yes, quite." Tristan shifted on the lounge chair. "I was wondering if you ladies would help me out in the Kid's Club until we can either track down Emerald or get another youth staff member flown out to join the cruise."

Hayley bolted upright, "Help you with children?"

Tristan nodded.

"Yeah. I'm afraid not. Have you met me?" Hayley raised her sunglasses and glared at Tristan. "No watching kids for me. I spent my childhood raising my brother and sister. I've watched enough kids to last me the rest of my life."

Tristan's shoulders sagged.

Hayley's voice raised. "And why are you asking us? Because we're women?"

Tristan sat up straight. He glanced around the pool deck to see if any of the passengers had heard Hayley's accusation. "Absolutely not. I'm asking you because, as entertainers, you have the most free time of the staff on board." He gestured at them laying on the lounge chairs by the pool.

"Oh. Sorry." Hayley winked her nose. "Can't you get the cruise staff to take turns running the Kid's Club?"

Tristan gestured at the crowded pool. "We're at full capacity this cruise. They are already spread thin. I can't cover all the activities and the Kid's Club with my staff."

Hayley rubbed her forehead.

"I've talked with Home Office. You'd be paid a stipend in addition to your entertainer salaries."

Hayley crossed her arms. "Nope."

"I could request a bonus as well as a stipend."

"There is not enough money in the world, Tristan Waterson."

Rachel leaned forward and lifted her sunglasses. "How much? I don't make as much as these two. I'm just a dancer, not a headliner."

Tristan told her. "And you can keep any tips and the babysitting fees."

"That's not too shabby. But what are you going to do when I'm dancing in the shows?"

Tristan looked at Olivia pleadingly. "Well, that's why I hoped that the three of you would help me out. That way, one of you could cover the Kid's Club when the other two had shows."

Hayley rolled her eyes and looked at Olivia.

Olivia sighed. "How many kids are onboard this cruise?"

Tristan looked down at his lap and mumbled. "Forty-seven."

Olivia leaned in and cocked her head. "How many?"

"Forty-seven."

Rachel threw herself back on her chaise lounge. "Yeah. Not sure there's enough money to watch forty-seven kids for a week."

One kid playing in the pool splashed his sibling. Water shot out of the pool and sprayed Tristan. He brushed the water off of his white shorts.

Tristan took a deep breath, "But they won't all be there at the same time. Their families will drop them off for a bit and then pick them up."

Hayley shook her head. "We have plans in port this cruise. I have some shopping I need to do in St. Thomas. My sister is moving, and I promised I'd get her some table linens as a housewarming."

Olivia chimed in. "And we booked an excursion already in Jamaica."

"The kid's club is closed when we're in port!" Tristan pleaded.

Olivia sighed, “I want to help you out. It’s just, I don’t think it is a good idea for me to be away from Chico that much. He gets anxious if I leave him too much. Then he doesn’t perform as well in the show.”

“Bring him with you!” Tristan lit up. “You said that the kids loved him. Bring him up to the Kid’s Club with you! He’ll be a hit with the children.”

Hayley glared at Tristan. “You’re just not going to give up on this, are you?”

Tristan shook his head, “I’m sorry. I really need your help.”

“I will not wear that stupid uniform. Who thought horizontal stripes were a good idea?” Hayley rolled her eyes.

“I’ll try to round up some youth staff t-shirts. You don’t have to wear the uniform when you are off duty. I promise."

Rachel shrugged. "I have to wear the cruise staff uniform anyway, so it doesn't bother me."

Hayley leaned forward, and her eyes narrowed as she looked at Rachel. "Have you seen the youth staff uniforms? They look like something a clown would wear."

Tristan wiggled his eyebrows and patted Hayley's leg. "I'm sure you can make the youth staff uniform look good."

Hayley rolled her eyes.

"So you'll help me?"

Hayley looked at Olivia and Rachel. They shrugged. "We'll help out for a day or two, but you need to work on getting someone to replace us asap."

Tristan exhaled and closed his eyes. "Thank you. I promise to make it up to you."

"You'd better."

Tristan reached into his pocket and pulled out pieces of paper. He handed one to each of them. "Here is the schedule of activities for the week in the Kid's Club."

Olivia looked it over and made a face. "Why does it have to start so early? We have shows at night and then we have to take down our props and pack them away. This is going to be miserable."

"Maybe Rachel can cover the morning shift after your magic show since she's not in it? Then you and Hayley can have a lie in after your late night." Tristan looked at Rachel pleadingly.

Rachel shrugged. "Sure."

Tristan looked at his watch and stood up. "I have to get going. You can work out the details. I'll come check on you this evening."

He turned away from them.

Hayley called to him. "Hey, Tris! Might want to change your shorts. Your boxers are showing!" She winked. "Stripes today, huh?"

Tristan ran his hand over his backside. "Good to know. Maybe the hand dryer will help." He walked over to the bathroom near the pool and pushed the door.

The door was locked.

He walked over to the enormous blue wheeled bin of striped beach towels, picked up a beach towel, and wrapped it around his waist. "Good thing most of the passengers do not know who I am yet!"

The girls giggled as he walked towards the elevator, gripping the towel around his waist.

"If only I didn't think he looked so darn good in his striped boxers, I could have turned him down." Hayley's head sank. "Ugh! What did we just agree to do?"

"It's just for one cruise. It'll be okay." Olivia pulled her beach bag out from under her chair. She fished out her flip-flops. "Ready?"

"Ready might not be the right word, but I guess we have to go." Hayley picked up her bag.

Olivia tied the shoelace on her sneaker, stood up, and looked at herself in the mirror. She closed her eyes and shook her head. "Hayley was right. This is horrendous."

"Holy moly!" Chico flipped upside down in his cage. "Uh oh!"

"Uh oh is right." Olivia shrugged. "It's just a few days, right?"

Someone knocked on Olivia's cabin door.

"Who is it? Come in!"

"Stop it, Chico! You know you're not supposed to answer the door!"

Olivia peaked through the peephole. All she saw was wide red and white stripes. She opened her cabin door. "Hey, Hayley. Come on in."

Chico squealed. He rocked back and forth, hanging from the roof of his cage. "Hey, hey, Hayley! Uh oh, oh no!" He hooked his beak to the bar of his cage and flung himself down to his perch. "Oh, my."

Hayley sighed. "Thanks, Chico. I was hoping it didn't look as bad as it felt. But you have clarified that it is truly awful, even upside down. Are you ready?"

"Yes, I think I'll wait to bring up Chico until we know what we're dealing with."

"Can you wait to bring me until you know what we are dealing with? I'll just stay here with Chico."

"Ah, Hayley. It'll be fun."

Hayley folded her arms across her chest.

"Okay, we'll make the best of it."

"I hope Tristan knows I wouldn't do this for any other human being on this planet."

Olivia grinned. "Hayley likes Tristan! Hayley likes Tristan."

"Are you five?"

"Just giving you practice for dealing with five year olds."

"Yeah, I have had more than enough experience. Thanks." Hayley sighed. "Let's get this over with."

Hayley pulled out the chair behind the desk. “I’ll check the kids in and give them their wristbands.”

Olivia looked at Rachel and then down at the schedule. “I guess that leaves us with coloring pages and puzzles until the welcome party starts at 7pm.”

Rachel shrugged, “Okay.”

Olivia pulled out bins until she found a stack of papers with outlines of cruise ships and sea animals. “Want to color a dolphin?”

“Oh good! You’re here!” A parent stood at the gate. “I was worried after this afternoon that there wouldn’t be anyone here.”

Hayley unlatched the gate and ushered in a little boy who looked about seven. She wrote his name on a wristband and put it on his wrist.

"Jimmy, be good for the girls." The mother looked at Hayley. "What time do you close?"

Hayley looked up at the clock over the door. "9pm."

"Oh, I thought you had babysitting until 1am?"

"Uh, yes, we do. That's an extra fee."

"Excellent, see you then!" She turned around and walked away.

Hayley, Rachel, and Olivia looked down at Jimmy.

Hayley walked behind the desk and plopped into the chair.

Olivia held up a coloring page. "Do you like dolphins?"

The little boy shrugged. He pointed up at the television on the wall. "What's that?"

"That's a television, but it isn't TV time right now. We're going to color while we wait for more friends to come play."

Jimmy fell to the ground and kicked the floor. "I want TV! I want TV!" He thrashed around and screamed.

Olivia's eyes were like saucers. She looked at Hayley.

Hayley walked over to Jimmy and knelt down next to him. "If you keep screaming, we won't turn on the television ever. Do you understand me?"

Jimmy froze. He looked at Olivia and kicked again.

Olivia looked at Hayley.

"Hey. What did I say?"

Jimmy shrugged. He stood up and took a piece of paper from Olivia and walked over to the tables by the windows. Jimmy pulled out one of the little chairs and sat down. He took a crayon from the basket in the center of the table and colored in the shark.

"How on earth did you do that?" Olivia shook her head. "Do you have super powers?"

"No, I just had two annoying little siblings."

Another parent stood in the doorway and Hayley walked over to the gate to greet them.

Within minutes, coloring children filled the chairs and Olivia had run out of blank coloring pages. She looked up at the clock above the door and down at the schedule in her hand. "Rachel. It says it is time for the ball pit, slide, and other fun. I do not know what this means. Have you seen a ball pit? Or a slide?"

Rachel and Olivia opened up cabinets until they found one full of big toys. They started pulling out plastic slides and bags of colorful balls.

Olivia lurched forward as a child ran into her from behind. "Whoa there!"

"Give me that!" Jimmy grabbed the bag of balls out of her hand and dumped them on the floor.

The children swarmed Olivia, grabbing the balls off the ground and throwing them at each other. Jimmy ran around the room grabbing as many balls as he could carry.

"Stop!" Olivia shouted over the chaos. "Jimmy, no running in the Kid's Club. Put the balls in the ball pit!"

Olivia and Rachel stooped to pick up the balls. A little girl kicked the ball Olivia was reaching for. Olivia stood up and put her hands on her hips. A ball hit her in the face.

"Ouch! Stop it! Someone is going to get hurt!"

The children kept throwing the balls at each other. One little boy sat on his bottom sobbing after a ball whacked him on the head.

Hayley stood up and walked into the center of the mess of children. She raised one hand high in the air. "Quiet!"

She cupped her ears with her hands. "Listening ears!"

The children all put their hands behind their ears and quieted.

"Let's see who can get the most balls in the ball pit the quickest!"

The children scrambled on the floor grabbing armfuls of the balls and dumping them into the ball pit.

Olivia sidled up to Hayley. "How on earth did you do that?"

Hayley sighed and rolled her eyes. "Way too much experience with children." She walked back over to the sign-in desk and sat down.

Some children jumped in the ball pit, others went down the little plastic slide, and a couple of children sat on the foam mats and built things out of cardboard bricks.

Olivia exhaled. She walked over to the tables and picked up the pictures the kids had colored and put them on the bulletin board by the door for their parents to see when they came to pick up their kids.

Tristan knocked on the door frame. "Hello all. Looks like things are going swimmingly!"

"At the moment. It was touch and go for a bit." Olivia nodded at Hayley. "Thankfully, she got them under control."

"That's my girl!" Tristan gave Hayley a tight smile.

Hayley pressed her lips together and raised one eyebrow.

"Alright then. I'll be on my way." Tristan looked down at his watch. "I have Trivia in five minutes."

Tristan turned on his heel and sped down the hallway. He turned and looked with wide eyes back at Olivia standing by the gate.

Olivia bit her lip to hide her smile. She turned toward the desk. "I think that man is terrified of you."

"Good." Hayley crossed her arms and leaned back in the hard plastic chair.

"Hopefully, he'll never ask me to do this again."

"Ah, Hayley. It's not like he didn't have any youth staff on purpose. It's not his fault that Emerald vanished."

Hayley gestured towards Rachel. "I can't say I blame Emerald for getting fed up and taking off."

The children were jumping up, trying to grab a toy out of her hand. She held it above her head. "One at a time, please!"

Olivia rolled her eyes and walked over to Rachel. She took the toy from her and put it behind her back. "Time to clean up!"

The kids groaned. Jimmy threw a ball at her.

Olivia ducked. She looked over at Hayley. "Let's see who can fill up the bag with balls the quickest!"

Rachel held up the empty bag. The kids started throwing the balls in.

Olivia looked at the schedule and her shoulders relaxed. "Hayley, it's time for a sing-a-long. Since you are a professional singer, can you lead this?"

Hayley stood up. "I'd love to, Livy, but Rachel and I have to head out."

"Head out? You're leaving me alone with them?" Olivia's voice quavered.

Hayley patted her back and pointed at the clock above the door. "We've got the Welcome Aboard show tonight. If we don't leave now, we won't have time to get changed into our costumes. And I am not going on stage in this outfit." She plucked at her oversized red striped shirt.

Olivia's shoulders slumped.

Hayley patted her shoulder. "You'll be okay, kid."

Olivia blinked slowly as she watched Rachel and Hayley lock the gate behind them. They waved at her and took off down the hallway.

Olivia closed her eyes and took a deep breath.

Olivia held the picture book up and slowly moved it from side to side so every child could see the picture. "And they lived happily ever after. The End."

She closed the book and put it down on her lap. Someone was standing at the gate waiting to be let in. Olivia jumped up. She pulled out a bin of blocks. "Who likes to build things?"

The kids lunged for the bin and dumped it on the floor.

Olivia raced across the Kid's Club to let the parent in.

She slowed.

It was Alex.

He rubbed his shadowed chin. His eyebrows shot up as he recognized Olivia. "Hey. I was doing my rounds and spotted you. Why are you in here? And why are you wearing that outfit?"

Olivia plucked at her oversized striped shirt. "It's a look, isn't it?"

"If anyone can pull it off..." Alex shrugged. "Did you get demoted from entertainer to youth staff?"

"Tristan asked Hayley, Rachel, and I to help since Emerald....."

Alex rubbed the back of his neck. "When I saw the Kid's Club open, I was kind of hoping she was in here with the kids and I just hadn't been informed. My staff and I have been combing the ship for her."

"Any luck?"

Alex shook his head. "No, not yet. But it's a big ship. Hopefully, we can track her down soon. We're checking to see if she got off the ship and didn't notify us. I'm hoping there was a mixup, and she flew home. But we still have possession of her passport."

"I hope she's okay."

"Me too." Alex looked at the remaining children sitting on the mats building block towers. "They're well behaved and they look like they are having a good time. You must be a natural with kids."

Olivia's hair fluttered as she exhaled forcefully. "You weren't here an hour ago. It was absolute chaos."

Alex chuckled. "Glad I missed it. Looks like you have it under control now."

"Thankfully, a lot of the parents came and picked their kids up after the first seating showtime, so I only have a few left." Olivia pulled the schedule out of her pocket. She breathed a sigh of relief. "Thank goodness. Movie time!"

"He hit me!" A little girl yelped.

"Gotta go."

"Good luck." Alex watched Olivia walk back over to the children.

She took the block out of the little boy's hand before he could lob it at another child, picked up the little girl, and held her on one hip.

"Jimmy! We don't throw things at our friends."

Jimmy ran around Olivia, a block in his hand, ready to launch it at her.

"No running, Jimmy. Give me the block." Olivia took the block out of his hand.

She opened up a cupboard and pulled out a stack of pillows with one hand. "Everyone, come get a pillow and a blanket. It's movie time!"

The children raced up to Olivia to get their pillows.

Olivia hugged the little girl. She looked at her name on her wristband. "Isabella, help me pick out a movie, alright?"

Isabella nodded, her thumb firmly wedged in her mouth. Her enormous brown eyes blinked sleepily.

"Getting tired?"

Isabella frowned. "No!" She mumbled with her thumb still in her mouth.

Olivia laughed. "Good, because we have a movie to watch." She walked over to the television, picked up the remote, and turned on the movie Isabella had chosen.

Jimmy groaned, “This is a stupid movie.”

“If you’re a good boy during this movie, maybe you can pick out the next one.”

Jimmy fell back on his pillow, his eyes glued to the screen.

Olivia laid Isabella down on the mat and tucked a blanket over her. She dimmed the lights in the Kid’s Club and threw herself down into the hard plastic chair behind the desk.

Irena parked her cart outside the door and opened the gate. She lifted a package of toilet paper. “Restocking your bathroom.”

“Thanks for bringing extra toilet paper for us.” Olivia nodded towards the kids.

"One of the little ones unrolled an entire roll onto the floor."

"Oh, goodness."

Olivia shrugged. "Could be worse. At least they put it on the floor and didn't flush it all."

"True." Irena glanced at the children laying on their mats. She put her hand on the gate. "You have a full house tonight."

"Yes! We have a lot of kids signed up for babysitting tonight. It is going to be a long night."

"That stinks. Hopefully, they will get picked up early." Irena opened the gate. "Is there anything else you need before I go?"

Olivia shook her head. "No, I think we're good."

Irena shut the gate behind her and pushed her cart down the hall.

Over the next couple of hours, parents picked up their children until only Jimmy and Isabella were left. Olivia kept glancing up at the clock above the door, dimly glowing in the darkened room. Time was moving so slowly, Olivia wondered if the clock was broken.

She looked at her watch. The time matched. Olivia sighed. The sigh turned into a yawn. Her eyes watered. Olivia was used to being up this late, but it had been a long day and sitting in a dark room wasn't helping to keep her awake.

Olivia tensed expectantly every time she heard footsteps in the hallway.

Five minutes before babysitting ended, Jimmy's mother showed up at the gate startling Olivia.

She must have dozed off.

Jimmy's mom brushed past Olivia, picked up Jimmy, and headed out the door without saying thank you or goodbye.

Olivia was used to the passengers being excited to see her when they recognized her from the magic show. It felt weird to be completely ignored.

Olivia shrugged and latched the gate. She sat down behind the desk.

The movie ended and went to static. She got up and turned the television off, plunging the room into complete darkness, the only light coming from the hallway.

Isabella stirred on the mat and sat up groggily. She wobbled as she looked around the room. Her whimper turned into a sob.

"Hey, it's okay. I'm here."

Isabella reached up with both arms, expecting Olivia to pick her up.

Olivia bent over and picked up the little girl.

Isabella clung to her, her head tucked under Olivia's chin. Olivia grabbed a blanket from the cupboard and tucked it around the little girl.

Isabella's sobs lessened. Her breath caught, she let out one last cry, and settled into sleep on Olivia's chest.

Olivia gingerly sank down into the hard plastic chair. She looked up at the clock above the door. It was five minutes after one in the morning. Isabella's parents were probably just running late.

Olivia kissed Isabella's head, breathing in the little girl's baby scent. She rocked her back and forth.

Olivia glanced up at the clock. She was sure her parents would pick up their little one any moment now.

Olivia jolted awake. She'd dozed off holding Isabella. She blinked and looked at the glowing clock through bleary eyes.

"Ugh. Where are your parents, Isabella?" Olivia whispered to herself. She looked up the little girl's cabin number and called. "Maybe they laid down for a minute and fell asleep."

The phone rang and rang. No one answered.

Olivia checked the list again, making sure she hadn't dialed the wrong room. She called again.

Still no answer.

Isabella fussed in her sleep.

Olivia rocked her back and forth until she settled again. She stretched her aching back and wiggled in the seat.

Annoyance turned to anger as the clock ticked closer to three in the morning. Olivia had to be back at the Kid's Club in less than six hours.

At five minutes past the hour, she called Isabella's cabin again.

Still no answer.

Olivia scribbled a note.

Olivia stood up, holding Isabella tightly to her chest. Not much was open at this time of night. Her parents must be in the Casino or the Disco.

Olivia unlatched the gate with one hand and walked out of the Kid's Club. She stuck the note to the bulletin board just outside the Kid's Club door. If Isabella's parents finally showed up, Olivia wanted to make sure they didn't leave and go looking for their child.

She took a couple of steps and then paused. The floor felt like it fell out from under her feet as the ship rode a wave. She was usually pretty confident with her sea legs, but carrying the sleeping child put her off balance.

Isabella's hot breath warmed Olivia's neck. The toddler snuggled deeper into Olivia's arms-er brunette ringlets peeking out of the blanket Olivia had tucked over her to protect her from the lights in the ship as they walked through the brightly lit ship looking for her parents.

She hesitated in front of the elevator, trying to decide if she should go up to the Disco or down to the Casino.

Olivia's shoulders ached from Isabella's weight. Isabella was just a toddler, but she seemed to get heavier as Olivia carried her. Olivia hiked her up.

Olivia watched the lights for each of the floors light up above the elevator as the elevator climbed up to the Pool Deck.

She widened her stance as the ship rode another wave, knocking her off balance.

The elevator door opened.

Olivia winced at the bright light in the elevator. She bent her knees, trying to reach the elevator buttons without waking Isabella. She grazed the button with her knuckle. Olivia leaned against the wall of the elevator as the doors shut.

The groan of the ship cutting through the waves echoed in the empty metal elevator as it swayed with the motion of the ship.

She closed her eyes.

The elevator lurched to a stop.

Olivia pulled away from the wall and waited for the doors to open.

The elevator settled a few inches, and the door opened.

Olivia stepped over the apron of the elevator and onto the deck.

Her arms felt like they'd stretched from carrying the child. She squeezed Isabella tightly and headed down the dark passageway towards the low hum of music.

Olivia slowed and squinted wondering why someone would have left a pile of clothes on the floor in the middle of the passageway. She wondered if bedding had fallen off of a cabin steward's cart or a family had dropped towels they'd taken from the pool.

Olivia shifted Isabella to her other side.

She squinted to see what peeked out from the bunched up red and white striped fabric.

Legs.

It wasn't a pile of bedding or pool towels.

It was a person.

Olivia took a step back, shook her head, and blinked.

She walked closer, hoping she was seeing things.

"Hello?" Olivia took a step closer, "Are you okay?"

She wasn't.

A halo of dark curls splayed out around the facedown figure.

Olivia nudged the person's hand with her foot, "Please wake up."

She gripped Isabella tightly to her chest and nudged her again.

No reaction.

The air hissed out of Olivia's lungs.

She gripped Isabella and bolted towards the elevator. Olivia punched the button, and the doors opened immediately. She tried to pick up the phone, but Isabella stirred in her arms.

Olivia pushed the button for the Promenade Deck.

As soon as the elevator door inched open, Olivia slid through and raced into the Kid's Club. She sunk down into the chair.

Isabella whimpered in her sleep. Olivia rocked her back and forth, making shushing sounds.

Olivia picked up the phone and dialed Alex's number.

"Ballas." His voice was gruff with sleep.

"Alex?" Olivia's voice quavered.

"Yeah. Who is this?"

"It's me. Olivia." Olivia's throat tightened. "Alex, there's a body up on Deck Ten."

"What?" He asked groggily. "What are you talking about, Liv?"

"Alex, I need you. I'll explain when you get here. I'm in the Kid's Club."

Olivia held the phone, afraid to put it down.

Isabella sighed in her sleep.

Olivia stood up and rocked back and forth from foot to foot, not sure if she was doing it to comfort the toddler or herself.

Heavy footsteps pounded towards the Kid's Club.

Olivia's eyes brimmed with tears as Alex's face appeared above the gate. She exhaled. Her voice shook, "Thank goodness, it's you."

Alex fumbled with the lock on the gate. He finally got it open. His white uniform shirt fluttered away from his bare chest as he crossed the brightly colored carpet of the Kid's Club and pulled Olivia and Isabella into his arms. He kissed the top of Olivia's head and rocked them back and forth as sobs poured out of Olivia.

He held her out at arm's length. "What on earth are you still doing here at 3:30 in the morning? And why do you still have a child?"

Isabella's head pulled away from Olivia. Her hair was matted to her head with sweat. She blinked groggily and took a deep breath, as if she was about to wail.

"Olivia?"

"Shh!" Olivia paced back and forth, shushing to soothe the child.

Alex buttoned up his shirt and tucked it into his pants.

Isabella settled back into Olivia's arms. Isabella's body weighed heavily in her arms as she settled back into sleep.

"What is going on?" Alex stalked around the room, opening closets and looking behind the toys. "You said there was a body."

Olivia's voice trembled,"Not here. Isabella's parents never came to pick her up. I called their cabin multiple times, but they didn't answer. I figured they had to be on the ship somewhere, so

I carried Isabella and was going to go looking for them."

Olivia explained how she had come upon the body.

"Sit down with the baby. I'll be right back."

"No!" Olivia shrieked. She lowered her voice. "Take me with you. I don't want to be here alone."

Alex closed his eyes. "Liv. I'll just be a minute. I'll radio Victor to come be with you."

Olivia lurched towards Alex. Her eyebrows furrowed. "Please."

"You have the child."

"What if... what if they come down here and.." Tears crested her eyes and ran down her cheeks. "I don't want Isabella to get hurt."

Alex looked up at the ceiling. "Fine. But you stay right behind me. If I tell you to do something, you do it immediately. Understood?"

Olivia nodded.

Her stomach felt like it dropped out of her body when the elevator whirred to life and whizzed upwards.

Olivia's eyes darted back and forth as she followed Alex out of the elevator and towards where she had found the body.

Alex stood with his back to the wall next to the corridor and gestured for her to be quiet and stay still as he readied himself to turn down the passageway.

Olivia nodded. Her neck ached from holding Isabella and the tension.

Alex pivoted out into the passageway.

He paused.

He looked at Olivia, his eyes narrowed. He raised a finger, "Stay here."

Olivia's heart pounded as she lost sight of him around the corner. She leaned back against the wall, the metal railing helping to support Isabella's weight.

She peeked around the corner.

Alex marched towards her. "Are you sure it was this deck?"

Olivia nodded.

"Olivia. There isn't a body. Nothing here."

Olivia swallowed, "What?"

"Are you absolutely sure it was this deck?"

"Yes! I was going to try the Disco first. Then go down to the Casino."

Alex ran his hand over his bristly chin. "We'll check the other decks, but there isn't anyone here."

Olivia breathed in, ready to argue.

"Liv, see for yourself." He took her by the upper arm and pivoted her into the passageway.

Olivia took a few steps forward. It was empty.

The crew door swung open.

Olivia gasped and lurched back, pressing her back to the wall.

Alex touched her arm. "Olivia. It's Victor. I radioed him to meet me here." He led Olivia to a bench across from the elevator and explained the situation to Victor.

Olivia felt a hot rush of shame and her cheeks flushed red when Victor glanced at her during Alex's briefing.

Victor nodded and took off.

Alex walked over to Olivia.

“He’s going to check the other decks. If he finds anything, Victor will report to me.” He knelt down in front of Olivia and rested one hand on her knee. “Let’s see if we can find this baby’s parents, okay?”

Olivia nodded. She couldn’t look at Alex.

“Do you need me to carry her?”

Olivia shook her head, “No, I don’t want her to wake up and be scared.”

Alex nodded and stood up.

Olivia struggled to get up from the bench with the sleeping child in her arms.

“Are you sure?”

Olivia nodded.

“Okay.” Alex led her down the empty passageway towards the Disco.

Olivia’s eyes stung from lack of sleep and from holding back tears. She glanced at the spot where she had seen the body.

"Shouldn't you and Victor look for, oh I don't know, clues of some kind?" Olivia's eyes darted past Alex.

"We'll check it out. Maybe the person just had too much to drink in the Disco and was taking a little nap on the floor. It happens."

"No! I know what I saw. She was obviously dead."

"Liv, maybe your mind played tricks on you."

Olivia shook her head.

"Olivia, even I sometimes think I see someone or something that isn't there when I'm doing rounds late at night. The ship can be eerie when it is late and empty with the sounds of the engine and the waves echoing off the walls. It happens to everyone."

Olivia stomped her foot and hissed. "No Alex. I didn't imagine it. The body was wearing a red and white striped shirt just like the one I'm wearing. I tried to wake her, but she didn't move."

She took a deep breath to steady herself. "I think it was Emerald."

Alex paused, lips pursed. "If it was her, Victor and I will find her. Let's hope it wasn't. Let's hope your mind was just thinking about her going missing and filled in a shadow."

Lights flashed, and the music pounded as they neared the nightclub.

"If you come in with me, Isabella is going to wake up. Is there anything about the parents that you can tell me that will help me identify them?"

"When she dropped Isabella off, the mother was wearing a yellow shirt and had long dark hair." Olivia kissed the top of the toddler's head. "Kind of like Isabella's."

"There aren't many people still in the disco this time of night, so if she's in there, I should be able to find her." Alex led her to a bench near the bank of elevators.

Isabella stirred from the pounding base coming from the nightclub.

Olivia settled down and rocked the toddler back into a deep sleep.

Alex walked up to the bouncer at the entrance and put his hand on his shoulder. The bouncer looked over at Olivia and Isabella and shrugged.

Alex disappeared into the nightclub. He circled the Disco looking for the parents and then headed back to Olivia.

"No luck. Barrett said he just got back from dealing with someone who had too much fun and passed out in the pool bathroom, but he has seen no one that matches her mother's description. The bartender and the DJ didn't think she'd been in tonight, either. Let's try the Casino, okay?"

Olivia nodded, her eyebrows pinched together. "I'm sorry."

"Sorry about what?"

"I woke you up and dragged you out of bed for nothing."

Alex stopped and turned towards Olivia. He took her shoulders into his hands. "Don't be sorry."

Olivia looked down at the gold and blue patterned carpeting and sniffled.

He lifted her chin with his fingers and raised it up so she was looking into his deep brown eyes. “Olivia Morgan, you are never bothering me. Understand? Day or night. For any reason.”

Olivia’s blue eyes glistened as she nodded.

He cupped her chin with his hand. He leaned in and then stopped as he looked at Isabella between them. “Let’s check the Casino. If they aren’t there, how do you feel about adoption? We might have a kid.”

Olivia’s breath caught as a laugh bubbled up.

Alex put his arm around Olivia’s shoulders and squeezed her close. “What would Chico think about being a big brother?" Alex punched the elevator down button, put his hand on the small of Olivia's back, and led her in.

There were still a few people at the slots and tables, but the Casino was emptier than Olivia had ever seen it before. She scanned the room from the doorway. “I think that’s them. See the woman in the yellow shirt at Anna’s table.”

“I see them. I’ll go talk to them.”

“Wait!” Olivia rocked Isabella back and forth. She kissed her head, again. Her breath was ragged as she exhaled. “I feel awful turning this sweet child over to them. Can you imagine just abandoning your baby overnight like this?"

"No Liv, I can't. But you can't keep her."

"I know. I just..." Olivia squeezed Isabella close and rocked her back and forth. Her shoulders shook and her cheeks puffed out as she exhaled.

Alex put his arm around Olivia's shoulders and squeezed her to him. "Isabella is a lucky child that you were watching out for her. Are you ready?"

Olivia looked up at him and nodded.

They crossed the casino. Isabella stirred from the noise and bright lights, but didn't wake up.

The woman in yellow caught sight of Olivia and saw the child in her arms. The smile faded from her face. She hunched down over her cards, avoiding looking at Olivia and Isabella.

Anna slowly looked from Olivia and the toddler in her arms to Alex and stopped dealing cards. “Officer Ballas? Is something wrong?”

“Anna.” Alex nodded at her. “This little girl’s parents didn’t pick her up at the end of babysitting tonight.”

Anna’s eyes darted towards the couple at the table.

The woman in yellow rolled her eyes. “Sorry we were late coming back. Here, give me the kid.”

“Ma’am. Children under 18 aren’t allowed in the Casino. You’ll have to come out to the lobby.”

The woman sighed.

“Now, ma’am.”

She gathered up her chips, elbowed the man next to her. “Let’s go. We’ve got to get the kid.”

Anna gathered up the cards on the table.

"Thank you, Anna." Alex stood behind the couple while they gathered their things, and then he and Olivia followed them out to the lobby.

The mother grabbed Isabella out of Olivia's arms when they reached the lobby and glared at Olivia. "She would have slept all night if you hadn't dragged her down to the Casino."

Isabella looked blearily around and wailed.

"See what you did?" The woman spat at Olivia.

Tears rolled down Olivia's cheeks as the woman walked away with Isabella. "That poor child."

"You did the right thing. She had no reason to talk to you like that."

Alex pulled Olivia into his arms. “Now, let’s get you to bed. I’m sure Chico is wondering where you are.”

Olivia pulled away from Alex and nodded. She pulled her damp shirt away from her shoulder. She stood up straight and shook her blond hair out of her face. “Sorry, I’ve fallen apart on you tonight.”

“You had quite a night. It’s fine.”

Alex’s radio blared to life. “All clear, sir. We found nothing out of the usual.”

“No sign of Emerald?”

“No, sir.”

Alex stuck the radio back on his belt.

Olivia pulled her shoulders back. “There was a person there.”

“Well, there isn’t one now.” Alex shrugged. “I don’t know what to tell you.”

“You don’t believe me?”

Alex rubbed his temple. "It's not that I don't believe that you think you saw something. But there wasn't anyone there when I came up and my team has found no one on the ground on any other deck."

"Thanks for helping me find Isabella's parents. Sorry I woke you up. I'll see you tomorrow." Olivia turned away.

"Don't be like that." Alex took a long step to catch up to her. "Let me walk you to your cabin. I want to make sure you're safe. Look, I'm not saying that you didn't see a body. I just don't know what you want me to do if I can't find a body."

Olivia stopped walking and hung her head. "Ugh. I forgot. The Kid's Club needs to be locked up. I'll see you tomorrow."

"I'm not letting you go on your own."

"I can take care of myself, now that I don't have Isabella to worry about. I'll be fine."

"I know you can take care of yourself, but I'm still going with you."

She looked at her watch. "You have to be on duty soon. Go get something to eat."

"No. I'm going with you."

"Fine."

"Wow."

"I know it's a mess. I didn't have time to pick up the mats and toys. Once Isabella fell asleep in my arms, I wasn't picking anything up."

Alex shook his head. “No, not that. Look.” He pointed out the window of the Kid’s Club.

A sliver of orange and pink along the horizon split the ocean from the sky.

“One benefit to being up this early is the sunrise at sea.” Alex grabbed her hand and led her towards the door to the back deck. “We won’t get any sleep, anyway. We might as well enjoy the sunrise.”

“You have to be on duty soon and you haven’t even had breakfast.”

“Olivia, I can always grab something to eat. The sunrise is fleeting. Come on.” He pushed open the door.

They passed the kiddie pool, crossed the deck, and leaned against the railing. The sun reflected on the wake of the ship as it broke the surface of the water.

Olivia took a deep breath of the salt air. She held it for a couple of seconds and then let it out. She yawned.

Alex put his arm around her shoulders and pulled her close.

Sea birds flew behind the ship and then dove into the churning water of the wake. One bird pulled up a fish that looked too big for him. He struggled to take off under the weight, but finally lifted off from the water and flew away. Other birds flew after him, trying to take his fish.

Olivia pointed. “Look! He got one! I guess he’s got his breakfast.”

“Let’s hope he can keep it.”

“Silly birds. There is an entire ocean filled with fish, but they’d rather go after their buddy who has one and take his.”

Pink cotton candy colored clouds floated in the sky.

Olivia sighed.

"It's beautiful, isn't it?"

She nodded. "Sometimes I wonder if I should quit ships and move back home. Get a normal job. But then I see a sunrise like this and I don't know how I could ever quit."

"One of the main perks of the job, for sure."

Olivia looked up at Alex. "Do you ever think about going back home and getting a regular job?"

Alex shrugged. "Not really. Between my time in the Navy and then on cruise ships, I've spent most of my adult life at sea. I don't even know what I would do. Plus," Alex gestured at the pink and orange reflecting off of the water, "I can't imagine a better way to start my day. Well, maybe one better way."

Alex turned towards Olivia and looked in her eyes. He put his hand on her cheek and tipped her chin up as he leaned down to kiss her.

Olivia pulled back.

Alex took a step back. "Sorry. I thought you wanted me to kiss you."

"I do!"

"Then why did you pull away? Am I reading your signals wrong?"

"No. I don't know. It's not you. I'm just not ready for this." Olivia closed her eyes. "It wouldn't be fair to you."

"Fair to me?" Alex's eyes bored into Olivia's. "How on earth would kissing you not be fair to me?"

"I'm not a fling kind of woman."

"Who said I'm looking for a fling?"

"Shipboard romances don't last." Olivia looked down at the wake tumbling behind the ship. "I might not even be here in a month. I still haven't heard if my contract will be renewed."

"Of course they'll renew your contract."

"Tristan says he's happy with the magic act, but I don't know if the show is good enough that they will give me another contract. It's expensive to ship out another illusion act. Maybe that is why they kept me on when Peter ditched."

"You're getting great reviews. Tristan was telling me how proud he was of Hayley and you and the show you've put together."

"That's nice to hear, but it isn't just up to him. Home Office might want a more experienced act."

"You are experienced. You've been doing magic on ships for years."

"It was always Peter's act. Not mine."

"Do you want another contract? It sounds like you might want to get off of ships?"

"I… I don't know. Being a magician wasn't my dream. It was Peter's." Olivia held her hair back as the wind blew it in front of her face. "I had this plan for my life. Peter and I were going to get married, and we'd work on ships for a few years. Then we'd get a casino job or something and have kids and I'd stop doing the show. Now none of that is going to happen and I don't know what I want my future to look like. I don't want to go through what happened with Peter again."

Alex jammed his hands in his pockets. "I'm not Peter. I would never do something like that to you."

"I didn't think Peter would do that to me."

"Don't lump me in with that.... philanderer. You can't put Peter's bad behavior on me." Alex's cheeks flushed red. "I'm not that kind of guy."

Olivia took a step towards him and laid her hand on his chest. The charm bracelet with the charm of Chico Alex had given her slid down her wrist. She outlined his gold name tag with her finger. "Oh Alex, I know you're not like him. It's me. I just need to get myself together before I bring anyone into my life."

Alex leaned on the railing and watched the birds diving into the wake.

The sun broke the surface of the water. The golden light reflected off of Olivia's face. "But it is hard to give up this life."

"Yes, this is an addictive way to live, isn't it?"

"Yes." Olivia sighed and looked into Alex's eyes. "It is hard to walk away from a job that gives you moments like this one."

The sky brightened to a pale blue.

Alex stepped back from the railing. "We'd better get the room cleaned up. I need to get ready to report to duty."

Alex pulled the mats off the floor, folded them up, and tucked them in the closet while Olivia grabbed the toys scattered around the room and put them in the bins.

She yawned. "Other than the hour or so I slept in the chair last night, I've been up for twenty-three hours. It is going to be a long day."

"Wait, you fell asleep in that chair?" Alex pointed at the orange plastic chair behind the desk.

"Briefly. I was holding Isabella and must have dozed off for a bit."

"Maybe you dreamed you saw a body?"

Olivia paused, a stuffed animal clutched in her hand. "What? Are you saying I imagined it?"

"No, not imagined, really. Maybe you dreamed it."

"Alex, I wasn't dreaming. There really was a body."

"You were exhausted, and we'd been talking about Emerald going missing. You are filling in for her. Maybe your mind took you to a bad place when you were asleep." Alex shrugged.

"I didn't imagine anything. It wasn't a dream. I saw a body." Olivia put her hands on her hips, the stuffed animal's feet dangled off her hip.

Alex held a mat in front of him. "I'm just saying we didn't find a body. If you dreamt it, that would explain it."

"I didn't dream it." Olivia's eyes flashed.

Alex tucked the last mat into the closet. "Okay."

"Don't patronize me. I am telling you I saw a body."

"I believe you." Alex's gaze swept the room. "Anything else we need to pick up? It looks pretty good to me."

"No, that's all."

"Liv, don't be mad."

"I'm not mad." Olivia unlatched the gate and walked through.

Alex latched the gate behind him and sped up to catch her.

"You don't need to walk me to my cabin. It's broad daylight now. You don't need to babysit me. I can take care of myself.

I probably just dreamed it all anyway, right?"

Alex groaned. "Olivia, I'm walking you to your cabin."

"Suit yourself."

He followed her down to her cabin.

Olivia swiped her key card and opened her cabin door. "Sorry, I woke you up for nothing."

"It wasn't nothing. Look, we're still looking for Emerald. I'll talk to Victor and the rest of the team at our morning meeting. If I learn something, I'll let you know. Okay?"

"Yeah."

"Helllloooo?"

Alex laughed. "Is that my buddy?"

Chico peaked out of the hole he'd chewed in his cover. "Treat?" He eyeballed Alex through the hole.

Olivia held the door open. “In a minute Chico.”

“Snack?”

“I said in a minute.” Olivia walked over and pulled the cover off of Chico’s cage.

“Looks like I’m not the only one ready for breakfast.” Alex laughed. “Maybe I’ll bring you something later. Okay, bud?”

“Okay, bud!” Chico danced back and forth on his perch.

“Take good care of our girl, alright?”

“Aye, aye, cap’n!” Chico squawked.

Alex pulled her cabin door shut behind him.

Chico climbed off of his perch and pushed on the latch of his cage with his beak. “Nuts?”

“I’m not nuts!” Olivia barked.

“Treat.” Chico stomped his foot.

"Oh. Yeah." Olivia opened the drawer where she kept his treats and pulled out an almond in the shell. She opened the latch on his cage.

Chico pushed the door open and climbed up on top of his cage. "NUT!"

"Yes, sir." Olivia handed him the nut. "I have an hour until I have to be back at the Kid's Club. Any chance you can eat your nut quietly and let me take a nap?"

"More nut!"

"Fine." Olivia pulled out a couple more almonds and popped them into his dish. She pulled the red striped shirt over her head, dropped it and her shorts on the floor, and climbed under the covers of her bunk.

She closed her eyes.

Olivia sat up and punched at her pillow, fluffing it up. She laid back down and closed her eyes.

She turned on her side and raised her arm over her head.

Her thoughts buzzed around in her head.

She flipped on her back.

"Ugh." Olivia sat up. "Have you ever been so tired you can't sleep, Chico?"

Chico sat on the perch on top of his cage, working on his nut.

"I saw a body in the passageway. I did."

"Uh oh."

"Exactly. Uh oh." Olivia flung herself back on her pillow. She closed her eyes. Alex's face appeared behind her closed eyes. Her heart fluttered as he leaned in. She sat bolt upright. "I need to find

Emerald, or at least figure out what happened to her."

Chico dropped the shell of his almond and gnawed away.

"You're not much help."

Olivia rubbed her face. She put her feet down on the floor of her cabin and reached for her youth staff uniform. She held up the limp red striped shirt. "I sure hope Tristan comes up with some t-shirts today."

"Sorry I'm late." Olivia hoisted Chico's travel cage above the gate.

"There you are! I was worried about you. You are never late." Hayley jumped up from the chair behind the desk and rushed over to open the gate. "What the heck happened to you? You look awful."

"Thanks." Olivia put Chico's cage on the desk. "Not sure anyone looks good in red and white stripes."

"Well, that too." Hayley looked Olivia up and down. "Seriously, what is wrong?"

"I had an awful night last night." Olivia quickly filled Hayley in on her late night.

"Hmph." Hayley nodded towards the children sitting in a circle on the mat in front of Rachel as she read them a story. "Isabella's father was in line to drop her off before we even had the sign-in sheet on the desk."

Olivia's head jerked towards the kids. "Nice. Not sure why they even brought her on the cruise."

Hayley shrugged. "Built in babysitting?"

"Anyway, Chico was alone all day yesterday, so I figured I would bring him with me. Hopefully, the kids will enjoy having him here."

"I'm sure they will." Hayley cleaned off the top of the bookcase behind the desk. "Here, let's put him on this so the kids can't put their fingers in his cage. We don't want anyone getting bit."

"He'd be more likely to fall to the bottom of his cage and cower in fear at the intrusion of a little finger, but good idea."

They got Chico settled.

Hayley pulled out the schedule. "We have half an hour until they deliver pizzas for the kids' snack."

"Snack!" Chico shouted from his cage.

Olivia groaned.

"Sorry!" Hayley laughed. "I forgot that was a sensitive word. Want to introduce Chico to the kids?"

Olivia nodded. She opened Chico's travel cage and held out her hand. "Ready to meet some new friends?"

"Hello!" Chico waved his foot up and down.

"Save your tricks until you meet them."

Olivia caught Rachel's eye and held Chico up where she could see him.

"Friends! We have a surprise for you!" Rachel stood up. "You remember Olivia? She brought a friend to meet you!"

Olivia carried Chico to the front of the circle of children.

The kids jumped off the mats and ran towards Chico, their hands reaching up, trying to pet him.

"Holy Frijoles!" Chico yelped.

The kids shrieked with excitement when Chico talked.

"Yikes!" Chico flapped his wings, climbed up Olivia's arm to her shoulder, and burrowed into her hair.

"Hold on! Everyone sit down." Olivia tried to get Chico to step on her hand, but he wouldn't come out of her hair. "Chico is nervous. Can you all sit quietly on your bottoms so he isn't afraid of you?"

Most of the kids sat back down on the mat. Jimmy made squawking noises and pretended to be a bird, flying around the Kid's Club.

Olivia looked at him and crossed her arms. "We'll wait until everyone settles."

Jimmy plopped down on the mat.

Once the children were quiet, Olivia reached into her hair and pulled Chico out. “His name is Chico. He’s an Amazon parrot.”

She lifted Chico up so the children could look at him. Jimmy jumped up and tried to pet Chico. Chico growled at him like a dog. Jimmy pulled his hand back. The children giggled and shouted, “He thinks he’s a dog!”

“Jimmy, I need you to sit on your bottom and stay there. Chico has a powerful beak. We don’t want him to get stressed or he might bite.”

“He talks?”

“He does! He also does some tricks. Would you like to see them?”

A chorus of yeses rang out.

“Chico, can you say ‘hello’ to the children?”

Chico turned his head and eyeballed the children.

"It's alright. They will stay seated." Olivia raised her eyebrows. "Won't you?"

The children nodded.

"Hello!"

The kids waved and said 'hi' back.

Olivia gave Chico a shelled sunflower seed. "Chico, can you show the children your tail?"

Chico slowly turned around on Olivia's hand. He looked over his shoulder at the children. When he was sure they were all sitting down, he shook out his tail feathers and then held them fanned out.

"Oooh!"

Olivia directed Chico to turn back around. "Would you like to do a dance with Chico?"

The children nodded.

Olivia took a step back. "Okay, everyone. Stand up."

Once they were on their feet, Olivia took another seed out of her pocket. "Put your left foot in!"

Chico raised his left foot and held it up high in the air. The kids giggled as they raised their feet.

"Shake it all about!"

Chico wiggled his foot up and down.

"And turn yourself about."

Chico turned around on Olivia's hand as the kids spun in circles.

"Good job!"

Olivia stepped off the gangway onto the pier and sighed. She walked alongside Hayley and Rachel, closed her eyes, and turned her face up to the sun. "A day out in St. Thomas is so much better than being stuck in the Kid's Club all day."

"Truth!" Hayley raised her hands.

"I will never take my life as an entertainer on a cruise ship for granted again after the past couple of days."

Hayley nudged Olivia with her shoulder. “We’re pretty spoiled, aren’t we?”

“Apparently, I mean, I know we work hard at our shows and put in a lot of time rehearsing, plus long days setting up and late nights tearing down our props, but it isn’t anything compared to spending an entire day entertaining two dozen little kids.”

“Ha!” Hayley burst out laughing. “My mother tried to convince me to study to be a teacher. She said that there wasn’t any security in being an entertainer. But the past couple of days have convinced me I made the right decision. I am not cut out for this line of work.”

“I’m not enjoying the long days, but I’m actually enjoying the little kids. I swear, I was pretty tempted to keep

Isabella when her parents never showed to pick her up." Olivia shrugged. "She's precious."

"Yes, she is. But for every Isabella, there is a Jimmy. He reinforces my commitment to not having children."

"Jimmy is a little terror. Did you see him swing that chair at me?" Olivia rubbed a darkening bruise on her thigh. "Thank goodness he's short and just hit my leg."

"Ouch!" Rachel winced.

"Hey, ladies! You need a ride?" The driver leaned against his taxi at the head of a line of cars.

"No, thanks!" Hayley shook her head.

"Always seems like a good idea to walk on the way into town, not always as good of an idea on the way back to the ship."

"The exercise is good for us. I have a list a mile long of stuff to buy today."

Hayley patted the pocket that contained her to do list. “Top priority is getting my sister’s housewarming gift. I need to drop it at the post office before we leave port today.”

Olivia paused and looked at a large lizard sunning himself on a rock. She looked up. Hayley and Rachel turned the corner past the shops.

Olivia waved goodbye to the lizard and raced to catch up.

“Slow down!” Olivia panted as she struggled to keep up with Hayley and Rachel. “Some of us don’t have long dancer’s legs.”

They walked through Havensite and turned left towards Charlotte Amalie. Hayley slowed as they passed the yacht club. The sun gleamed off of the white boats lined up in a row in the sparkling turquoise water. The water in the bay glistened like diamonds were floating on the surface.

Hayley put her arms around Olivia's and Rachel's shoulders. "So, instead of going back on the ship and watching rugrats for the rest of the week, maybe we rent a yacht and cruise the Caribbean on our own."

"Do you even know how to sail?" Olivia shielded her eyes from the sun with her hand and looked at Hayley. She raised both hands. "Why am I even asking? No, we're not going to ditch the ship. Tristan would be livid."

"Tristan is the one who got us into this."

"It isn't Tristan's fault that Emerald is missing."

"No, of course it isn't. I didn't mean to imply that." Hayley tucked a copper colored curl behind her ear. "I'm just annoyed that he asked me to bail him out. If he and I weren't... you know... would he have asked?"

"I think you're being too sensitive. He asked all three of us. And he is right. We have more available time than any other staff on the ship."

"I guess you're right, Liv. I felt pressured." Hayley shrugged. "Like he was expecting me to help because of our personal relationship. We're not that serious. It's just supposed to be a little fun. You know what I mean? Shipboard romances don't last."

"Hey!" Rachel raised her eyebrows.

Hayley laughed. "Except yours, my dear. I'm sure you and Nigel will grow old together. But you have to admit, it is the exception, rather than the rule. Most ship romances don't last."

"That's what I told Alex."

Hayley reached in front of Olivia and stopped her. "Hold up. You told Alex what, exactly?"

"That shipboard romances don't last." Olivia shrugged.

Hayley's eyes narrowed as Olivia's eyes darted away.

Hayley grabbed Olivia's and Rachel's hands. "Sounds like there is something you need to spill. Let's get something to eat while you tell us everything." Hayley looked both ways. Olivia took a step forward, and Hayley pulled her back. "Watch out! Traffic is on the other side of the street today."

After the van passed, Hayley pulled Rachel and Olivia through the crosswalk to the other side of the street. They climbed up the stairs of a cheerful yellow restaurant overlooking the harbor. They placed their order at the counter and grabbed a table by the railing of the balcony.

Olivia swirled her straw through her frozen cappuccino.

"Are you sure you don't want a rum punch?" Hayley took a sip of her drink and eyed Olivia. "I feel like we'd get more details if you had a rum punch."

Olivia raised her eyebrows. "It seems a little early in the day for a rum punch."

"It's brunch. People drink Mimosas and Bloody Marys, what's wrong with a rum punch?" Hayley raised her plastic cup. "Cheers."

Olivia took a sip of her coffee and gazed past the palm tree at the small boats lined up at the Port Authority Dock, their ship visible in the distance.

"Spill it, sister."

Olivia stabbed a potato and took a bite.

"Quit stalling." Hayley glared at Olivia. "Why were you and Alex discussing shipboard romances?"

Olivia swallowed her bit of potato salad. "Nothing happened."

"Nothing happened? I'm afraid I don't believe you." Hayley's eyes narrowed. "What do you think, Rach?"

"Did Alex kiss you?" Rachel grinned and raised her plastic cup towards Olivia.

"No!" Olivia sat bolt upright in her white plastic chair.

Hayley's eyes widened. "Oh! He wanted to kiss you, though, didn't he?"

Olivia's shoulder's sank as she took another sip of her frozen cappuccino.

Hayley's hand covered her mouth, then she raised her pointer finger and jabbed it toward Olivia. "And you wouldn't kiss him."

Olivia tapped her cup on the table to break up the ice in her frozen drink.

Hayley leaned in. "Am I right?"

Olivia slouched in her chair. "Maybe."

"What is wrong with you?"

"Nothing is wrong with me."

Rachel bit her lip. "If I wasn't with Nigel and Alex wanted to kiss me, I sure wouldn't say no."

Hayley clinked her plastic cup to Rachel's. "Exactly. So tell us what happened."

Olivia filled them in. "I don't even know how long I'm going to be on the ship, so what's the point in starting a relationship?"

"Not every kiss has to lead to a relationship. You can just kiss the hot guy because you're standing in front of a beautiful sunrise and it would feel good." Hayley wiggled her eyebrows. "Kissing good-looking men is one of my favorite things to do."

"That's awesome for you." Olivia laughed. "It just isn't me. Besides, I'm happy on my own. I've been in a relationship for a long time. It is good for me to figure out what I want and not look to a man to find direction in my life."

"That is an excellent point. But I still vote for kissing."

"Eat your croissant, and let's change the subject away from kissing."

"You are no fun at all."

"So I've been told," Olivia popped the last bite of her brie and fig sandwich into her mouth, "By you, mostly. So what is on our agenda today? I want to give my mom a call while we're in port."

"My sister is moving into her first house. I need to get her a present and get it in the mail since I won't be at her housewarming party."

"Sorry, you're going to miss it."

"I'm not. I think she's too young to settle down to a mortgage payment." Hayley drank the last of her rum punch. "I tried to get her to get a job on a ship, but she says she likes her job. I don't know why she'd rather work in a bank and have a mortgage than live like this."

Olivia gazed out at the boats bobbing in the water. She sighed. "This is pretty amazing. But I can see the charm of having your own place and building roots."

"I'm thinking that I'll get her a set of everyday tablecloths and a Christmas set." Hayley held up two tablecloths. "Not like I'll be hosting holidays in my studio apartment or on the ship."

Olivia ran her hand over the white set Hayley had set aside. "I love the cutwork on this one. And the Christmas set is very festive. I think she'll love them both."

"Good. Then we can get out of here and I can get these in the mail to her." Hayley looked back and forth between Rachel and Olivia. "I need to get a card."

They walked a block down Main Street and turned onto an alley lined with shops. Olivia ran her hand along the rough brick wall. Pots of tropical plants were grouped around the doors to the shops in the narrow alleyways. Hayley led them to a small store and looked through the racks of cards.

Olivia picked up a wooden box with a parrot painted on the lid. "Rachel, look at this! It looks just like Chico!"

"It does. You need to get that."

"I do. What should I put in it?" Olivia took the lid off and looked inside the box.

"Chico would vote for treats."

"You got that right. But the artist signed this. I think I need to think of something better than treats to keep in it."

Rachel ran her finger over Olivia's silver charm bracelet and held the parrot charm in her hand. "You could keep your jewelry in it."

"I never take this off." Olivia adjusted the bracelet. "But I have other jewelry I could put in it."

They paid for their purchases and headed into the narrow alleyway.

Hayley held up her shopping bags. "I'm ready to go to the post office. Or do either of you need to stop anywhere else while we're in town?"

Rachel shrugged. "I have some postcards I want to mail, too. Would you mind if we stopped at the health food store after? I'd like to get some snacks for the week. Between working in the Kid's Club and the shows, I don't have enough time to get snacks."

"Great idea." Hayley shifted her shopping bag to her other hand. "I'm always up for some good snacks."

Olivia laughed. "If you two keep saying the word snacks, Chico is going to break out of the ship and fly into St. Thomas to find out what you have to offer."

"I've seen that bird fly. I don't think he could fly all the way into town." Hayley pretended to walk like a penguin. "Maybe he could waddle to the health food store, though."

"I'm sure I can find some goodies for him at the health food store so he can stay in our cabin napping and not worry about having to forage for himself."

"While you two go to the post office, I'm going to wait for you in Emancipation Park, if that is okay?"

"No problem. We'll come get you after we're done."

Olivia made her way to the park and found a bench in the shade near the Liberty Bell display. Tourists wandered in and out of the blue pop-up tents set up in the parking lot in front of the park and chickens scratched in the dirt next to her bench.

Olivia closed her eyes. The lack of sleep from the late night was catching up with her. Her head bobbed and jolted her awake. She rubbed her eyes and yawned.

Her stomach growled as the smell of barbecue wafted past. Olivia leaned forward to look at the food trucks lined up around the parking lot to see where the smell was coming from.

Olivia caught sight of a flash of a red and white striped shirt in the crowd next to the food truck. She grabbed her shopping bag, jumped off the bench, and crossed the park towards the figure in the striped shirt.

The person darted into the crowd of shoppers perusing the booths, looking for a last minute souvenir before they headed back to the ship. Olivia saw a halo of curls bobbing in the crowd.

"Emerald!" Olivia called over the ruckus of the crowd.

The person crossed the parking lot and headed towards Fort Christian.

Olivia sped up, trying to catch her. "Emerald!"

Olivia climbed the grade of the hill to the rusty red seventeenth century fort. She reached the crest just in time to see the striped shirt enter the main door of the fort. Olivia raced to catch up. Olivia darted around a chicken pecking in the dirt at the base of the tree shading the forts' entrance and burst through the arched doorway into a wide open courtyard.

The stone and brick-paved courtyard was lined with green arched doors every few feet, each framed in sand colored brick. Some were open, but the green shutters on most were closed.

Olivia crossed the courtyard, glancing in the open doorways, hoping to glimpse the missing youth counselor.

A flash of movement in one of the open rooms caught Olivia's attention.

She crossed the courtyard. A family of tourists examined a display of artifacts.

No one wore a striped shirt.

Olivia shielded her eyes as she went back out into the sunny courtyard. She peeked into each entrance as she passed, but there was no sign of Emerald.

The wrought-iron gate creaked as Olivia pulled it open. A blast of damp air hit her as she passed through the thick brick walls. She held her breath as she entered the dungeon.

No one was there. She shivered and goosebumps popped up on her arms.

She walked back out into the courtyard, scanning the fort for Emerald. She spotted stairs going up to the roof.

Sweat trickled down her neck as Olivia's feet pounded up the stairs to the roof of the fort.

Olivia circled the roof, peeking in the turrets looking for Emerald. They were all empty. She crossed to the water side of the fort. She jerked her hand back as she touched the sun heated barrel of the cannon pointed towards the harbor.

Puffs of white clouds hovered over the turquoise water. Two flags in the grass oval below snapped in the wind. The breeze blew Olivia's hair behind her and dried her sweat.

No sign of Emerald.

She crossed the roof towards the courtyard and glanced at the clock in the tower. A flash of red and white stripes passed out of the door of the fort.

Olivia raced around the fort and down the stone steps. She dove out of the front door of the fort, hoping to see which way Emerald had gone.

"Where on earth have you been?"

Olivia jumped as Hayley grabbed her arm.

"We've been waiting for you. I finally left Rachel on the park bench and went looking for you."

"Did you see her?"

Hayley shook her head. "See who? Rachel?"

"No!" Olivia's head whipped back and forth, looking for Emerald.

"Emerald! I followed her into the fort. She had to have walked right past you when she left."

"I don't know, Liv. I didn't see anyone." Hayley waved to Rachel to come over and pointed at Olivia. "Are you sure it was Emerald?"

"Yes. I mean, I think so. I only really saw her from behind. She was wearing her youth staff shirt."

Hayley snorted. "Why would anyone wear that hideous uniform shirt off the ship when they could wear their street clothes?"

Olivia covered her mouth with her hand. "I don't know. I didn't think of that. Maybe it wasn't her?"

"Could've been a tourist with poor taste in clothes." Hayley shrugged.

"Could be."

Rachel caught up to them. "Ready?"

They popped into the health food store on their way back to the ship.

Rachel peaked into Olivia's shopping bag. "What did you get?"

"Some sunflower seeds and almonds in the shell for Chico."

"Motivation for him to entertain the kids?"

"I am willing to bribe him if it keeps the kiddos busy and happy."

Hayley's eyebrows shot up, and she tapped her chin. "Oh! I need to get Tristan to give me some bribes to finish out the cruise, doing youth staff duties. Margaritas by the pool when I'm off duty, or should I go for jewelry?"

Olivia looked down at her watch. "If you are going to ask for bribes of jewelry, you had better hurry before we leave St. Thomas. Lots of choices in jewelry stores here."

"That's the truth!"

They waited for a truck to pass and then raced across the road towards

Havensite. Their ship silhouetted above the shops.

Hayley reached out and put a hand in front of Rachel and Olivia. “Stop!”

Olivia’s heartbeat sped up. “What?”

“A hamburger and fries. Should we put off going back on the ship and get fast food?”

“You scared me over a burger?” Olivia shook her head.

Rachel held up her shopping bag. “I just spent a lot of money on healthy snacks. You want me to blow all of my good intentions on fast food?”

“You two are no fun.” Hayley stuck her tongue out at them. She pointed at the ship. “I’m going to need some kind of naughty treat before I go spend the rest of my day with all of those kids.”

"It's not that bad. You are being a real pip." Olivia rolled her eyes.

"I have put in my time watching kids with my brother and sister."

Olivia shrugged. "I'm enjoying being with the kids more than I thought I would."

Hayley stopped and turned Olivia towards her. She laid her hand on Olivia's forehead.

Olivia pulled away. "What are you doing?"

"Looking to see if you have a fever."

"I don't have a fever."

Hayley raised her eyebrows. "Baby fever?"

"For goodness' sake, Hayley."

"We're having so much fun doing the magic show together. You're not going to give this all up, are you?"

"My contract hasn't been renewed yet, so it might not be my choice."

"Tristan hasn't signed you on for another contract?" Hayley's eyes narrowed, and she put her hands on her hips. "He told me he loves our magic show."

"It isn't just the cruise director who decides on the headlining acts. The entertainment director has to want to keep me, too."

"Gayle loved our show. I'll have a talk with Tristan. Don't you worry about it, okay?"

Olivia nodded.

"You want to stay onboard, don't you?"

"Yes!" Olivia glanced up at their ship. "Of course I do."

"Good."

They came to the gate for their ship, but Hayley veered off.

"Where are you going?"

"I need fortification before tonight. And maybe a cocktail."

Olivia and Rachel followed Hayley to the restaurant at the edge of the dock.

"Livy, grab a table and Rachel and I will order, okay?"

"Sounds good. I still need to call my mom, so I'll do that while you order."

Olivia found an open table and put her bags down. She sat down facing their ship.

She dialed her mom.

The phone rang and rang. No answer. Olivia left a message.

She hadn't been able to get a hold of her mom since she'd left at the end of the last cruise.

Passengers streamed back to the ship, loaded down with shopping bags.

Olivia dialed her Uncle Mike.

No answer.

A woman in a red and white striped shirt walked down the Promenade deck of their ship. Olivia lifted her sunglasses and squinted at the receding figure.

Rachel carried over a rum punch for Olivia. "Since you didn't get one at brunch."

Olivia stood up and pointed. "Look!"

Rachel turned and shielded her eyes with her hand. "Look at what?"

"The person in the striped shirt on the Promenade Deck." Olivia wiggled her hand. "See her?"

Rachel squinted. "I don't have my glasses on."

Olivia slumped back in her seat. "Ugh! I was really hoping someone else would see her."

"See who?" Hayley put a plate of nachos on their table.

"Emerald."

"Oh! Where is she?"

"On the Promenade Deck. Or at least she was." Olivia exhaled. "At least I think it was her."

Hayley picked up a chip. "Do you think she's hiding to get out of watching the kids?"

"She could be, I guess." Olivia popped a jalapeño in her mouth and took a sip of her rum punch.

"Maybe I need to hide to get out of watching the kids for the rest of the cruise."

"Seems risky. It's only a week. You love working on the ship." Olivia took a sip of her rum punch. "If they find Emerald on the ship and she just didn't show up to work, she'd get fired. Why risk a regular gig?"

"Ha!" Rachel choked on her drink. "Maybe she knew that kid Jimmy was on board and couldn't face a week with him in the Kid's Club."

"Good point." Olivia glanced up at the Promenade Deck. "He's... challenging."

"That's one word for him." Hayley leaned back in her chair and raised her face up to the sun and closed her eyes. "I wish we had time to head to Magen's Bay. I am feeling beach deficient."

"Maybe next cruise we can plan to go there. I always want to plan a beach day when we're in St. Thomas, but I end up running errands instead." Olivia scooped up salsa and sour cream with her chip and ate it. Olivia drank down the last of her rum punch. She glanced back at the ship.

"Look! Do you see her?"

Hayley and Rachel whipped around. "See who? Emerald?"

Hayley squinted. "Yes, see the striped top?"

"No. I don't see her."

"Up there!" Olivia pointed at the receding figure.

Hayley followed where Olivia was pointing and scanned the ship and shook her head.

"I don't know why I'm even trying to look without my glasses." Rachel turned back towards the table.

Olivia reached into her pocket, got out her wallet, and threw some cash on the table. "I'll meet you on the ship. I've got to see if it is her."

Olivia raced to the gangway, pulled out her ID, and flashed it at Victor. "Did you see a woman with a red and white striped shirt come through here?"

Victor shrugged. "It's been pretty busy with the tour buses dropping everyone back."

Olivia ran to the crew stairs and took the steps two at a time up to the Promenade Deck. She pushed the door open and popped out on the walkway encircling the ship. Olivia walked briskly down the deck. A few passengers were sitting on the teak lounge chairs reading and others were standing by the railing looking out at St. Thomas.

No one was wearing the striped shirt Olivia had seen from shore.

Olivia looked down at the dock. Hayley and Rachel were walking towards the ship. Hayley had Olivia's shopping bag in her hand. She had been in such a rush, she'd left the bag with the wooden parrot box at the table.

Olivia circled the ship, looking at each person she passed, but there was no sign of anyone in a youth staff shirt. Olivia pushed open the door and headed back inside the ship.

"Irena!" Olivia waved at the cleaner.

Irena turned off her vacuum. "Yes?"

"Sorry to bother you. I was wondering if you saw someone in the red and white striped youth staff uniform?"

Irena shook her head. "No. Sorry." She went to turn her vacuum back on.

Olivia raised a finger. "Or a passenger in a shirt that looks kind of like that?"

"Sorry." Irena shrugged.

"Thanks."

Olivia walked down to the Purser's Desk. Sophie was helping a passenger. Once she was free, Olivia got her attention. "Sophie. Have you heard anything about Emerald?"

"Youth counselor, right?"

Olivia nodded.

Sophie looked around the lobby and leaned in. "You know I don't gossip."

"I know. Of course. I just thought you might have seen her."

"I haven't. Nell, that's her roommate, told me that Emerald had been seeing someone new, but she didn't know who." Sophie looked around the lobby again to make sure they were alone. "Apparently, she told Nell she was going to go to his cabin and never came back. Nell is worried sick about her."

"If you see Emerald, let me know, okay?"

"Of course, dear."

A passenger came out of the elevator and made a beeline for Sophie. Olivia backed away. She crossed the lobby and knocked on Alex's office door.

"Come in."

Olivia popped her head in. "Do you have a minute?"

Alex's face lit up. "Of course. Come on in. Have a seat."

Olivia slid into a chair across from his desk.

Alex shoved the paperwork he'd been working on out of the way and leaned back in his chair. "You got some sun today. I figured you'd have a nap this afternoon after last night."

Olivia shook her head. "I went into town with Hayley and Rachel. Tried calling my mom, but she didn't answer."

"When you talk to her, please tell her 'hi' for me."

"I will. So, the reason I came to see you..."

"Ah, so there is a reason you stopped by other than to see me?"

Olivia shifted in her seat. "Uh, yeah. I mean."

"It's okay, Liv. What's up?"

"It's about Emerald. I think I saw her."

Alex leaned forward. "You saw her?"

"I think so." Olivia filled him in on seeing Emerald at the fort and then on the Promenade deck. "But no one else saw her and I couldn't track her down to be sure it was her. Alex, do you think she could just be hiding out on the ship?"

"Her ID wasn't scanned coming on or off the ship. Are you sure it was her and not just someone wearing a shirt that looks like a youth staff uniform?"

"I asked Victor if he'd seen someone in that shirt come back on the ship and he said he hadn't noticed. Maybe he wouldn't have noticed if she'd scanned her ID"

"I have an alert set up on her ID. I would have been notified if we scanned her card."

"Oh." Olivia sunk down in the chair.

Alex stood up and walked around his desk. He sat on the edge and took Olivia's hand. "We have everything covered. If she is on the ship, we'll find her. If she scans her ID, I'll know it. You don't need to worry about it. Okay?"

Olivia nodded. She paused. "Have you talked to her roommate?"

"Liv, my team and I are doing everything necessary to find her." Alex squeezed her hand. "We've got it under control. I promise. Don't worry about it. You've got the kids to watch this cruise."

Olivia pulled her hand back. "I am capable of doing more than just watching children, Alex. I can handle doing two things at the same time."

Alex raised his hands. "Of course you can. I didn't mean to imply you couldn't."

"No running, Jimmy!" Olivia rubbed her temples and looked at the schedule. She clapped her hands to get the children's attention. "Guess what? It's pool time!"

Rachel, Hayley, and Olivia led the kids out onto the small deck behind the Kid's Club where the kiddie pool was located and helped them take off their t-shirts and swimsuit cover-ups. They rubbed sunblock on the kids and let them hop into the pool.

Isabella leaned against Olivia and wrapped her arms around her leg. Olivia knelt down. "Ready to play in the pool?"

The toddler clung to Olivia. Olivia gave her a hug. "Want me to come with you?"

Isabella put her thumb in her mouth and nodded her head.

Olivia reached down, took her hand, and led her to the baby pool. She lifted her up over the edge of the pool and plopped her into the water.

Isabella reached up for Olivia and stomped her feet in the water.

Olivia sat on the edge of the pool and put her feet in the water. "Is this better? I'm right here with you."

Rachel dumped a laundry basket of pool toys into the water.

Olivia picked up a little rubber fish and raced it through the water to Isabella. "Fishy, fishy!"

Isabella took the fish toy from Olivia and sat down on her bottom in the shallow water. She wiggled the little fish back and forth in the water.

Olivia ducked, but it was too late. A bucket of water came flying at her, drenching her. "Jimmy! Do not throw things."

Jimmy hopped out of the pool and ran across the pool deck to the little plastic slide.

Olivia squeezed the water out of her hair. "Walking feet Jimmy. No running." She shouted. She stood up. The red stripes of her shirt showed through her wet white shorts.

"Oh man. He really got you." Rachel made a face.

"Yeah. He really got me." Olivia exhaled. "We just have to get to lunchtime, right?"

"Yes, lunch. And then we have to get through the rest of the day."

"I always knew how hard the staff and crew worked, but after this cruise, I will have a new appreciation."

"Yes!" Rachel picked up a sock a child had left on the deck. "I will never whine again about having to work a shift at the library."

"Let me know next time you work and I'll come hang out with you."

"I promise not to splash you!"

"See! A step up from here!" Olivia raised her hand to her mouth. "Jimmy! No running. You can slip and fall and get hurt on the wet deck. Do you understand?"

Jimmy stuck his tongue out and wiggled his hips back and forth.

"Can we go to the library now?"

Hayley opened the door and pointed at her watch. "We need everyone back in their clothes and dry in twenty minutes."

Isabella picked up her fish and stood up in the pool. She climbed over the edge of the pool and headed towards the slide.

Olivia squinted. "What is wrong with her swimsuit?"

Isabella waddled to the slide. Her swimsuit bottoms were stretched out like she had a ball in them.

"Liv, was she in a swim diaper or a regular diaper?"

Olivia's eyes darted back and forth. "I didn't know there were special diapers for swimming."

As Isabella climbed the steps up the slide, her swimsuit bottom slid down under her swollen diaper.

Hayley shook her head. "It's amazing that there is any water left in the kiddie pool. I think her diaper soaked it all up."

Isabella reached the top step of the slide and plopped down on her bottom.

A damp exploding sound came from across the children's pool area.

"Oh, no." Olivia lurched forward.

Piles of white gel landed on the slide and on the pool deck.

Olivia ran towards Isabella, trying to grab her before she slid down the slide.

"No running!" Jimmy shouted at her as she caught Isabella up in her arms.

Olivia took a deep breath and ignored him.

Isabella's diaper was blown out in the back and chunks of gel fell out onto the ground.

Olivia held her out in front of her as she carried Isabella into the small bathroom off the Kid's Club.

She pulled out one of the extra diapers from the pile tucked in a basket under the changing table and cleaned Isabella up. "Oh girl. What a mess."

Isabell stuck the toy fish in her mouth.

"No!" Olivia grabbed it out of her hand and Isabella burst into sobs. "It was in the pool water. You can't put it in your mouth."

Olivia held the damp child to her chest and rocked her back and forth, soothing her. After she got Isabella calmed down, she dressed her and took her back out into the Kid's Club. The parents lined up at the doors to pick their kids up for lunch.

Jimmy's mom came to sign him out. "Did you have fun?"

Jimmy pointed at Olivia. "She's bad. She ran. We're not supposed to run, right Mommy?"

His mom whisked him out of the door.

Once all the kids had been picked up, Rachel, Hayley, and Olivia picked up the toys on the floor of the Kid's Club.

Hayley grabbed her stomach. "I'm starving. Thank goodness this morning is over!"

"Almost over," Olivia gestured towards the door to the kiddie pool. "We've got to clean up out there."

Hayley looked at the clock. “Great. We have to be back here in forty minutes. We’re not going to have much time to eat lunch.”

Olivia shook her head. “No, you and Rach go have lunch. I’ll clean up the mess. I might be a few minutes late coming back after lunch.”

“Take your time. We’ll hold down the fort until you get here.”

Olivia fished the toys out of the kiddie pool and washed them all off. She stuck the laundry basket of toys back in the storage closet and walked out to the slide. She shook her head, unsure of how to clean up the exploded diaper.

Olivia took the only broom she found in the closet and tried to sweep up as much of the gel as she could, but it just kept rolling across the decking.

She went back inside the Kid's Club and called the Purser's Desk.

"Chief Purser."

"Oh good, Sophie! It's me, Olivia."

"Hey mate. How are you?"

"I've been better. We had a diaper explosion in the Kid's Club. Can you send a cleaner to help me?

"A what exploded?"

"One of the kid's diapers." Olivia thought for a second. "A nappy exploded."

"Oh bless, of course. I'll send someone up right off."

"Thanks, Sophie."

Irena came up to the gate at the door. "Miss Sophie said you needed a cleanup?"

"Yes! Oh, thank you, Irena!" Olivia led her outside and showed her the mess. "I tried to clean it up, but it just kept rolling around."

"Cat litter."

"No, it isn't cat litter. One of the kid's diapers exploded."

"No, I mean I will put down cat litter. It will soak up the water in the diaper gel and then I can sweep it up."

"Oh, you're brilliant!" Olivia grinned. "Thank you so much!"

Irena smiled. "Thank you. That means so much. Not everyone is so grateful to us when we clean. I can't tell you how many times I came in here and they left the place a disaster. I had to clean up all the toys that had been left out before I could even vacuum in the Kid's Club."

"Oh, my goodness! That's awful. I can't imagine leaving the place a mess and expecting you to clean up the toys. That's not your job."

"Some people treat the cleaning staff like we aren't even human beings with feelings. I will go get the cat litter and be back soon."

"Do you need me to stay here and wait for you or is it okay if I go get lunch?"

"No need to stay. I can handle it all, just fine." Irena headed out. "Can you leave the Kid's Club unlocked for me?"

"Sure. Hey! Before you go. You haven't seen Emerald, have you?"

"Emerald?" Irena pushed the gate open. "Not for a few days."

"Have you seen her this cruise?"

"I do not know. Why?"

"She didn't show up for work this cruise."

"Sounds like something she would do."

Olivia cocked her head. "Why do you say that?"

Irena shrugged. "It just does." Irena shut the gate behind her.

Olivia's hair hung in damp tangles around her face as she took the crew steps down to the Officers' Mess to grab something to eat. Chunks of diaper gel clung to Olivia's shorts. The red stripes bled through her white shorts, leaving pink streaks.

Olivia grabbed a tray off of the stack and put a plate and silverware on it. She turned to pick up the salad tongs and bumped into another crew member, also reaching for them.

Bianca, the jewelry shop manager, jumped backwards, away from Olivia. “Ew. What happened to you?”

Olivia pursed her lips. “Got a little wet.”

“You look like you got a lot wet. What is that stuff all over you?” Bianca wrinkled her nose and took another step back. She brushed white gel off of her slim black skirt.

Olivia started to explain, but decided that telling Bianca about diaper gel wouldn’t help the situation. She shrugged.

Bianca took her tray and walked to her table.

Olivia closed her eyes and took a deep breath.

"You've got to be kidding me. I am not getting dressed up in a costume. This uniform is embarrassing enough." A hot flush of shame washed over Olivia as she thought of Bianca's reaction to her soggy, stained, diaper gel covered uniform at lunch.

Hayley threw her arm around Oliva's shoulder. "Come on. You'll be perfect!"

"Chico loves you, Hayley. He can sit on your shoulder while you're dressed up like a pirate."

Hayley shook her head. “He and I are buddies, but he’ll feel more secure with you. The kids will be excited and loud. He’ll be happier being close to you.”

“You are using my love for my parrot to get out of dressing up like a pirate?” Olivia glared at Hayley and then sighed. “Why do you have to be right? Ugh, I hate it when you’re right! He will be more comfortable with me.”

“At least you’ll get out of leading the kids through the ship. You and Chico will get to hang out by the Bridge together until they finish the scavenger hunt and find you.”

“Yeah, hang out dressed like a pirate. Super fun. Good try, though.”

“Just trying to look at the positive.” Hayley shrugged. She opened up the closet and pulled out a brown wooden pirate's chest.

Olivia lifted the lid and jumped back. "Oh, my goodness! I thought it was a dead animal!" She pulled out a brown curly wig.

Hayley took it from her and plopped in on her head. "Can't be a proper pirate without dark, curly hair!"

Olivia's bottom lip stuck out. "This just keeps getting worse and worse."

"You look adorable!" She tucked a loose blond strand up under the wig.

Rachel skipped down the stairs from the bathroom. "Oh!" She pulled to a stop.

Olivia turned towards Rachel. "It's me."

Rachel covered her heart with her hand. "Whoa! Well, that's a look."

Olivia glared at Hayley. "Apparently, I've been roped into dressing up as a pirate for the kid's scavenger hunt."

"Wow."

"Unless you want the opportunity?"

"Uh, no. Thanks though." She leaned towards Olivia and peaked into the wig. "Are you sure that thing doesn't have bugs living in it?"

Olivia whipped it off her head. "Yuck. I'll wear a wig cap under it for sure."

"Good idea." Hayley pulled out a long-sleeved red and white striped shirt, a vest, and pants and handed them to Olivia. "Go to your cabin, get changed, and get Chico. Rach and I will stash the treasure chest under the stairs by the Bridge. Okay?"

"Resigned." Olivia sighed. "I think that is the right word. I am resigned to my fate."

"See, you're sounding like a pirate already." Rachel patted her back. "At least you don't have to walk the plank."

"Hey!" Chico greeted Olivia as she entered her cabin.

"Hey right back. I've missed you this cruise." Olivia dumped the costume on her bunk.

"Treat?" Chico lifted his right foot and waved at Olivia.

"You know what, yes, you can have a treat." Olivia handed him a sunflower seed. "Want to go on an adventure with me?"

Chico dropped the shell and gobbled down the seed. "More treat?"

"Yes, there will be treats involved."

"Oooh, baby!" Chico shouted. He launched into a scale. "La, la la, la!"

"All of this alone time while I've been working has got you rested and raring to go, hasn't it?"

"Hmmm...snack?"

"We'll get to snacks. First, I need to get into this awful outfit." Olivia lifted the shirt up off her bed. "I just can't get away from these blasted red and white stripes!"

Olivia changed into the pirate costume and put a wig cap over her hair. She looked at herself in the mirror. "You could have a nice normal job. Work in an office.Wear pretty clothes to work every day. But here you are, dressed up like a pirate."

"Pie?"

"No, Chico. Not Pie. Pirate." Olivia slipped her foot into her boots and tied them up. She pulled the wig on her head and plopped the tricorn hat on top of the curls."

"Whoa, Nelly!" Chico ran to the back of his cage. "Aaaah!!!"

"It's just a wig, you silly bird." Olivia held out an almond. "Come here. Step up."

Chico raised a foot off the floor of his cage and then put it back down. He looked at Olivia suspiciously. His desire for the almond won out, and he stepped onto her hand.

Olivia pulled him out of his cage. "You know how I rarely let you sit on my shoulder?"

Chico warily studied the halo of curls on Olivia's head.

"Today is your lucky day, because parrots sit on pirates' shoulders."

Chico leaned back as Olivia lifted him to her shoulder. He cautiously stepped onto her shoulder, leaning away from her dark hair.

"Might as well go all out if I'm going to do this." Olivia took some of her black eyeshadow and brushed it on her face. She put in a gold hoop earring on the ear on the opposite side of Chico. "I don't need you pulling the earring out."

They passed a few crew members on their way to the elevator, but most of the crew members didn't pay them any attention. They were used to seeing strange things happen in the crew hallways.

Olivia and Chico took the crew elevator to the Bridge.

They had tucked the treasure chest under the stairs where Hayley had promised it would be. Olivia pulled it out and opened the lid.

The trunk was filled with small plastic toys and wrapped candies.

"Ooh! Treat!"

"This is candy. It isn't good for you, Chico." Olivia closed the lid and sat down on the painted metal steps, waiting for the kids to find her and Chico.

"La, la, la, laaaa!" Chico belted out a scale. His song echoed off of the empty metal hallway walls.

"Save it for when the kids find us, alright?"

"What are you doing?" Chico trilled. "What are you, what are you, what are you doing?"

"Waiting for the kids." A door opened around the corner. Olivia hunched down by the treasure chest in the cubby under the stairs.

Someone's shoes clicked along the bare floor. Whoever they were, they were too quiet to be the group of kids. Olivia popped out into the stairwell. "Oh."

Alex froze. He squinted. "Olivia?"

"The one and only."

He shook his head and chuckled. "Well, this is a surprise. I only realized it was you when I saw Chico."

"Hey, baby!" Chico shouted.

"Hey, yourself!" Alex reached into his pocket and pulled out an almond. He held it up. "May I?"

"Are you carrying around an almond in your pocket for Chico?"

Alex shrugged. “Gotta look out for my buddy, right?”

“Oooh!” Chico wiggled back and forth, shaking his wings.

“Can I give it to him?”

“You have to give it to him now. He’ll follow you around the ship until you do.”

“Excellent! Here you go, Chico.” Alex took a step toward Chico, holding out the nut.

Chico flapped his wings with excitement. Olivia’s wig blew across her face from the breeze he generated. The wig moving startled Chico, and he launched himself off of Olivia’s shoulder and landed on Alex’s hand.

“Snack?”

Alex grinned. “Of course!” He handed Chico the almond.

Chico grabbed the almond and perched on his hand, eating it.

Olivia shook her head. “He never goes to men.”

“Well, he came to me! We’re buddies, aren’t we?” Alex took in Olivia’s outfit. “So, what’s the deal with the pirate costume? Do I need to warn the Captain that we have a marauder on board?”

“I’m wearing this ridiculous costume for the kids. Hayley and Rachel are leading them on a scavenger hunt to find treasure.” Olivia gestured towards the chest on the floor behind her.

“You and Chico are treasures, so that makes sense.” He reached up to pet Chico’s back.

Chico whined a little and leaned away from his hand, but then went right back to eating his almond.

"Amazing. Chico never lets men touch him. I don't know exactly what happened before I adopted him, but he has always been afraid of men. He likes Joseph, but Joseph has never tried to pick him up. Chico wouldn't even let Peter give him a treat."

"Chico obviously has excellent taste."

Screams echoed off the walls and the sounds of little kids shouting and racing up the stairs bounced off the ceiling.

"Sounds like you are about to be discovered by a bunch of little treasure hunters."

"I believe you are correct."

Alex lifted Chico up to Olivia.

Chico hopped onto Olivia's hand. "Ahoy, matey!"

"Ahoy!"

Olivia put Chico on her shoulder and slid behind the trunk.

The noise grew louder as the kids stomped towards her hiding place. They rounded the corner wearing paper pirate hats and wielding paper swords.

Hayley shushed them. “You have to be quiet when you’re looking for treasure. You don’t want to give away any secrets!”

The kids quieted briefly before their excitement got the best of them and the volume went back up.

Rachel held up a piece of paper. “I found a clue!”

The kids encircled her, trying to read the clue.

Jimmy shouted, “I know, I know!” He raced towards the stairs.

Olivia jumped out and yelled. “Arrrr! Who’s coming to steal my treasure?”

Jimmy lunged at her with his paper sword.

Chico squawked. “Uh oh!”

The sword crumpled as it hit Olivia’s thigh.

Olivia lunged towards the kids. “Are you here to steal my treasure?!”

The kids screamed and ran towards Hayley and Rachel. Isabella started to whimper, and Rachel scooped her up and whispered in her ear.

Olivia leaned down. “If I share my treasure with you, do you promise not to give away my secret location?”

“Treat!” Chico yelled.

The children joined in, chanting, “Treat, treat, treat!”

Olivia opened the trunk and the kids dove in grabbing toys and candy. “Just one toy and one piece of candy each.”

Jimmy shoved a handful of treasure in his pocket. Olivia saw him but decided not to push the issue with him.

Isabella hung back, too scared of Olivia in her pirate costume to come closer.

Olivia pulled out a few gold foil wrapped chocolate coins and a plastic necklace and handed it to Hayley to give to Isabella.

Isabella grabbed them from Hayley and buried her head in Rachel's arms.

Hayley got the kids' attention. "Time to leave the pirate alone to guard her treasure. We have a party to go to!"

The children's shrieks echoed off of the wall.

"Argh!" Chico shouted.

"You're not helping, Chico."

Hayley led the kids away. She glanced back over her shoulder. "See you in the Disco after you get out of your outfit?"

Olivia nodded. She closed the lid on the treasure chest. When she turned around, she saw Alex leaning against the wall, looking at her.

"Oh!" Olivia hesitated. "I didn't know you were still here."

"I figured you might need security if the little pirates got out of hand."

"Everyone dance to the port side of the ship. Do you know which side is the port side?"

The kids looked quizzically at Rachel.

"It's your left side." Rachel held up her left hand.

The kids wiggled, but didn't move to their left.

Jimmy raced around in circles.

Hayley grabbed Olivia's hand and pulled her up front. "Let's show them how it's done!"

Rachel called out more dance moves while Olivia and Hayley led the kids in the dances.

"Let's see if we can make the ship bounce in the water! Everyone jump up and down!"

The kids all jumped up and down to the beat of the music.

Rachel pretended she was going to fall from the ship rocking back and forth. "Whoa! The ship is rocking and rolling!"

The kids jumped higher, giggling.

"Freestyle!" Rachel shouted into the microphone.

The children went bananas, dancing and wiggling to the music. Jimmy flopped to the floor and spun around on his back.

Olivia swept Isabella into her arms and spun her around the dance floor until she giggled uncontrollably.

Hayley and Rachel grabbed the hands of a couple of the children and danced with them in a circle.

Sweat trickled down Olivia's forehead as she carried Isabella around the dance floor. "Up?" Olivia lifted Isabella up into the air, as Isabella belly laughed.

"Me, me, me!" The kids grabbed Olivia's shirt and shorts to get her attention. She lowered Isabella to the ground and danced with a few of the other children.

Hayley tapped Olivia on the shoulder and gestured for her to follow her. Olivia left the kids dancing to the music.

"They're going to sleep well tonight!" Olivia shouted over the music.

“Me too. All this dancing makes up for not going to the gym this week.” Hayley pointed to the cake. “They are going to crash from the sugar in that frosting. Help me cut up pieces and put them on plates, please.”

“Of course.”

Hayley cut the cake and Olivia scooped the pieces onto small paper plates. She stuck a fork in each piece of cake. Once they had enough pieces cut up and plated, they gestured to Rachel to lower the music and lead the kids over.

Olivia handed out drinks to the kids as Hayley and Rachel took them each a piece of cake.

“Everyone sit on your bottoms and be careful not to drop your cake.”

A little boy leaned towards his slice of cake and licked the frosting off. "I don't like cake. Only frosting," He announced.

Olivia looked at Hayley and shrugged. "It's my favorite part, too!"

Hayley grinned as she licked the knife. "Not bad."

Jimmy jumped up, holding his plate filled with cake. "More!"

Olivia walked up to him. "Jimmy, you still have most of your slice of cake. Now sit down on your bottom before you spill it."

Jimmy dropped to the floor. His plate launched out of his hand and the cake went flying.

Oliva tried to grab it before it hit the floor.

Jimmy jumped up when he realized his cake was falling. His head collided with Olivia's face.

Olivia reeled backward, blood trickling down her chin. Warm blood covered her palm as she covered her mouth with her hand.

A gasp hissed out of the nearby children.

"I didn't mean it." Tears ran down Jimmy's cheeks. He threw the plate on the floor.

Olivia closed her eyes and took a breath. "I know you didn't. Rach, can you get Jimmy another piece of cake?"

Rachel scooped up another slice of cake for him.

"Jimmy stay on your bottom so you don't drop it, okay?"

Jimmy nodded.

Olivia bent down to clean up the cake. A little girl recoiled from her.

Hayley grabbed her shoulder and spun her around. "Let me see."

Olivia swallowed. The metallic taste of blood filled her mouth.

Hayley shook her head. "Your lip is really split. You might need stitches."

Olivia shook her head. "No, it's not that bad."

"Do you really want to take the risk of having a scar on your face?"

Olivia's shoulders sagged, "No."

"Then go see Dr. Kohli. He'll know what to do."

"I can't leave you and Rachel here all alone with all these kids."

"Go. We'll be fine." Hayley walked Olivia towards the door. "Their parents will pick them up in just a few minutes."

Barrett met them at the door. “Whoa! What happened to you?”

Hayley sighed. “Oh good, you’re here. Olivia got head butted by one of the kids and split her lip. Can you walk her down to the infirmary?”

Barrett looked into the Disco. “I’m supposed to be getting things set up for when we open.”

“I am perfectly capable of walking myself down.” Olivia waved Hayley and Barrett off, another gush of blood ran down her chin as she took her hand off of her mouth to talk. Olivia wobbled.

Barrett grabbed her arm. “No, she’s right. I’ll take you to Dr. Kohli.”

“Thanks Barrett. Keep an eye on her.”

“I will.”

“Back to the munchkins for me.” Hayley jogged back into the disco.

Barrett pulled out a handkerchief. "Here, you can use this to stop the blood."

"Thanks. You really don't have to walk me down. I know how to get to the infirmary."

"Ah, it's no big deal. I bring passengers down there a few times a week when they've had a little too much to drink." Barrett pushed the elevator button. "Lots of folks overestimate how much they can drink when the ship hits some waves. At least you're not going to barf on me. You're not feeling sick are you?"

Olivia shook her head. "No, you're safe."

Barrett sighed in relief as he punched the B Deck button. "Good. I've had some doozies this week, so it is good to know."

"Been a crazy cruise, huh?"

"Yeah. Some cruises you get bigger partiers than others. I had someone pass out cold, and a couple of women were in one of the bathrooms fighting a few days back. I also had to escort a few passengers to their cabins who couldn't stand up by themselves. It's always something. But that's my job, you know?"

"I think I'll stick to doing my magic show."

"Were you doing a magic show for the kids when you got hurt?"

"No, I'm helping out in the youth department this cruise."

"Lots of kids this cruise?"

"Yeah." Olivia slurred. "Sorry, my lip is swelling, and it is hard to talk."

The elevator opened and Barrett held the door open for Olivia.

She pulled his handkerchief away from her mouth. “I’m so sorry. I think I ruined it.”

“Aw, don’t worry about it. My mom sends me packs of them in every care package she mails me.”

“That’s sweet of her.”

Dr. Kohli looked up from his desk. “Goodness. What wild animal got you this time?”

“A wild animal named Jimmy.”

Dr. Kohli narrowed his gaze. “I am unfamiliar with that species.”

“Jimmy is a seven-year-old boy.”

Dr. Kohli nodded and laughed. “Ah, yes. As the father of five boys, myself, I am familiar with the damage they can do. Thank you for bringing Ms. Morgan to me, Barrett. I’ll handle it from here.”

"Yes, sir." Barrett waved to Olivia and headed out.

"Let me look at your injury."

"It's not bad. It's just bleeding a lot. You know how much stuff in your mouth can bleed. I wouldn't have bothered you, but Hayley wanted me to come."

Dr. Kohli pulled the handkerchief away from her lip. "Hayley was right. It is rather deep."

"I'm not going to need stitches, am I?" Olivia winced.

Dr. Kohli pulled an ice pack out of his freezer and handed it to her. "No, I believe a butterfly bandage will keep your lip together while it heals."

"I have a show tomorrow night. I can't have a bandage on my face."

Dr. Kohli held up a bandage. “It is tiny, my dear. No one will see it from the audience.”

“Can I take it off during the show?”

“My dear, you do not want it to scar, do you?”

Olivia shook her head. “No, I really don’t.”

“Then behave yourself and leave this on. I want to see you back here in two days so I can make sure it is healing and you don’t have an infection.”

“Yes, sir.”

“Now, that’s my girl.” Dr. Kohli applied the bandage and held up a small mirror. “See? It hardly shows.”

Olivia’s bottom lip was swollen to twice the size of her top lip and was already turning color. “Hardly.”

“Keep ice on it to reduce swelling.”

Dr. Kohli followed her to the elevator and pushed the button.

"You don't need to take me to my cabin."

"Of course, dear. I'm actually going on a hunt for a missing wheelchair. It was missing when I came into the infirmary the other day. I assumed someone would bring it back, but it looks like I need to make a report with your friend Alex."

"He's not my friend. I mean, he's my friend, but..." Olivia trailed off.

"Of course, my dear." Dr. Kohli winked at Olivia.

"It doesn't look that bad, Liv." Hayley stabbed a lettuce leaf and shoved it into her mouth.

"My lip is so swollen, I can see it when I look down." Olivia stuck out her lip. "And it is purple."

Rachel rubbed Olivia's shoulder. "It doesn't look as bad as it feels. I promise."

"Maybe we can put some purple lipstick on you and it will look intentional."

"I hope the swelling will be down by the time we do the show." Olivia cautiously slurped her soup. "Do you think we'll be able to cover the bruise with makeup?"

"I made a lot of fake bruises when I took Theatrical Makeup in college. I'm sure I can cover it."

"I hope so." Olivia held the ice pack up to her mouth. "Sorry I'm so slow at eating. I keep dribbling down my chin."

Hayley put her drink down on her tray and stood up. "Take your time. I'd say you should just take the entire night off, but we have the production show tonight so we can't cover babysitting. Do you want me to talk to Tristan and see if he can have someone cover for you when we have to leave for the show?"

Olivia shook her head. "No, everyone is busy. It'll be okay. The kids will just be watching a movie. I can ice my mouth there just as easily as I can in my cabin.

Hopefully, their parents will pick them up early tonight."

"Tristan said that if a parent doesn't pick up their kid at the end of babysitting, we can tell them they can't leave them with us again."

"Yeah, but I worry Isabella's parents would just leave her alone in their cabin after she falls asleep."

"I never thought of that. Why have kids if you don't want to take care of them? I enjoy having my freedom. That's why I don't plan on having kids." Hayley picked up her tray. "Don't rush. Rach and I will handle it until you get there."

Rachel put a dish of pudding in front of Olivia. "Chocolate pudding will make you feel better."

"Thanks. Love you both."

"Love you, too. Sorry you got hurt."

Rachel and Hayley put their plates in the dirty dish bins and headed up to the Kid's Club.

Olivia finished her soup. She licked her spoon clean and dipped it into her pudding.

"See you later, Nell." A crew member got up and left the Officer's Mess.

"Nell?" Olivia recoiled as she realized she'd said her name out loud.

"Yeah?" A small blond in a cruise staff evening uniform spun around and looked questioningly at Olivia.

"You're Emerald's roommate, aren't you?"

"Yeah." Nell looked Olivia up and down, taking in Olivia's youth staff uniform. "You work in her department?"

"Not really. I'm just filling in this cruise." Olivia winced as she bit her lip. "Do you have any ideas about what happened to her?"

"No. Not really." Nell shook her head. "She's probably staying in some guy's cabin."

"Why do you say that?"

"Because I told her she couldn't keep bringing back strange guys to our cabin."

"Oh. Yeah, I can see how that would be a problem." Olivia ate the last spoonful of pudding. "Did she leave all of her stuff?"

"That good-looking security officer came with some other guy. They took all of her stuff."

"Alex? I mean, Officer Ballas?"

"Yep, that's the one."

"Oh. If you hear from her, would you mind letting me know?"

"I'm pretty sure I'm the last person Emerald would seek out. But sure, I'll keep you in mind if I hear from her." Nell picked up her tray and headed out.

"You only have five left. They're settled in on the mats watching a cartoon." Rachel grabbed her tote bag. "Need anything before I head to the theatre?"

"No. Thanks for getting them settled for me."

"I hope the parents come and pick the kids up in a timely manner so you aren't here too late tonight."

"Thanks. I am pretty ready for today to be over." Olivia raised her ice pack to her mouth.

"If it helps, the swelling is down some."

"I think the ice is helping." Olivia nodded. "Break a leg."

Rachel headed out. Olivia sat down at the desk and pulled out her book. She adjusted the desk light to shine on the pages in the dimly lit room.

One by one, the parents came and picked up their children until only Isabella and Jimmy were left. Olivia tried to concentrate on her book, but she couldn't help looking up at the clock, hoping they'd show up.

Jimmy's mother came to pick him up at 11:30pm. She gathered her sleepy child up and carried him through the Kid's Club.

"I didn't do it." Jimmy pointed at Olivia's bandage on her lip.

"Of course you didn't, Jimmy." She looked at Olivia. "What happened to you?"

Jimmy's eyes widened.

Olivia touched her face with her hand. "Just an accident."

"You should really be more careful working with children. You need to lead by example."

Olivia took a breath. "Thanks for the advice."

Jimmy and his mother headed out, leaving only Isabella asleep on the mat.

Olivia walked over to the television and turned it off, plunging the room into darkness, and returned to her place at the desk.

The clock ticked closer to closing time.

Olivia read another chapter.

A light flashed across the windows of the Kid's Club. Olivia leapt up and ran to the door to the kiddie pool. She peeked out of the small round window in the door.

A flash of light skimmed the deck, pausing on the shallow pool.

Someone with a flashlight was walking back and forth across the deck.

Olivia shivered.

She put her hand on the door handle and then pulled it back.

The light vanished around the corner.

"Did they close up?"

Olivia jumped at the voice calling from the gate.

"You said they were open until two, right?"

"That's what that chick said."

Olivia crossed the Kid's Club. "I'm here. Isabella is sleeping on that mat by the windows. Let me turn a light on so you can get her."

Olivia slowly raised the lights until Isabella's sleeping form appeared.

Her parents crossed the room and scooped her up. Isabella looked at Olivia groggily as her mother carried her out of the Kid's Club.

Olivia breathed a sigh of relief.

She packed up her book and her now warm ice pack and put them in her tote bag. Olivia turned up the lights and picked up the pillows and blankets strewn around the floor of the room. She stripped the pillowcases off the pillows and threw them and the blankets into a trash bag for housekeeping to pick up.

She locked the door behind her and headed towards her cabin.

The empty corridors seemed filled with shadows after her late night scare the other night.

She breathed a sigh of relief when she reached her cabin without running into anyone.

Olivia pulled her key card out of her pocket and swiped it.

The light flashed red.

She swiped her card again.

The light flashed red.

Olivia leaned her forehead against her cabin door with a thunk.

"Hello?" a sleepy voice called out from inside her cabin.

"Chico. It's me. My card won't open the door."

"Come in."

"I can't come in. My key card isn't working." Olivia sighed.

"Who is it?"

"It's me, Chico." Olivia tried the key card again. Another red flash of light. "I wish you had opposable thumbs, buddy. You could let me in."

"You need to be let in?"

Olivia jumped at the voice behind her in the passageway.

"Joseph!" She laid her hand over her pounding heart. "What are you doing up at this time of night?"

"My supervisor woke me up. Nell, from the cruise staff, called him. Her toilet broke in her cabin. I'm on my way to see if I can fix it for her."

"He woke you up for that?"

Joseph shrugged. "Part of the job."

"I didn't know you were Emerald and Nell's cabin steward. Did you hear Emerald is missing?"

"Of course. Hopefully, she will show up soon."

"Do you think something bad has happened to her?"

"Oh, Miss, I hope not." Joseph's eyes widened. "Miss Nell said she probably just signed off the ship and they lost her paperwork."

Olivia cocked her head. "Nell said that?"

Joseph nodded.

"She told me she thought Emerald was staying at some guy's cabin."

Joseph shook his head. "No, not Miss Emerald."

"Why do you say that?"

"She is engaged to a man back at her home." Joseph crossed his arms.

"Wait, Nell told me Emerald was always bringing men back to their cabin."

"No. Not Miss Emerald." Joseph scoffed. He lowered his voice. "Can't say as much about Miss Nell. I clean their cabin. I know who has company and who does not. If you know what I mean."

Olivia nodded.

"Well, I had better get down to her cabin and see what the problem is."

Joseph scanned his master key card.

"Come in!" Chico grumbled.

The light flashed green.

Olivia opened her cabin door. She'd left the overhead light on in her cabin when she'd checked on Chico and brought him some carrots for a snack earlier in the day.

Chico peeked out of the little hanging fabric tent Olivia had made for him. "Goodnight."

"Sorry, buddy. Did I wake you up?"

Chico scooted back into his tent. "Goodnight."

"Alright, I get the point." Olivia switched on the night light over her bed and turned off the overhead light. "Is that better?"

"Snack?" He popped his head out of his tent.

"I'll give you an almond if you want to come out and cuddle with me?"

"Cuddle?" Chico slid out of his tent and waddled towards the door of his cage.

Olivia opened the door. "Up."

He stepped onto her hand. He tilted his head and looked at her lip. "Booboo?"

She reached up and touched the bandage on her mouth. “Yes, a little booboo.”

“Uh oh!” He rocked back and forth. “Oh, no!”

“It’s okay. It’ll get better soon.” She laid down on her bed and pulled Chico into her arms.

He snuggled under her chin while Olivia pet his head. The feathers on his neck fluffed up and his eyes closed. Olivia rubbed his neck and cheeks.

Chico made little contented noises with his beak as he settled in.

“Night, night.”

“Night, buddy.”

Olivia fished the key for the Kid's Club out of her pocket. She put the key in the lock and turned it, but the door wouldn't open. She put her key in the lock again and turned it the other way.

The door opened.

Irena knelt on the floor, rummaging through the closet. When Olivia stepped into the room, Irena jumped away from the closet.

"Hey." Olivia waved. "How are you this morning?"

"I didn't hear you come in." Irena put her hand on her chest. "I was just putting some toys away that I found when I was cleaning."

"Thanks! I'm sorry I didn't get them all last night. I must have missed them."

"It is not a problem." Irena closed the closet door, grabbed the handle of the vacuum and her bucket of cleaning supplies and carried them into the hallway.

Olivia pulled out a fresh sign-in sheet and taped it to the edge of the desk. She reached in her pocket and pulled out the schedule for the day.

Arts and crafts, games, free play, and then a tour of the Bridge.

At least there wasn't any cake. Olivia touched her face. Her mouth was still tender, but thankfully, the swelling was much better this morning and she'd been able to cover the bruise with makeup.

"Oh good! You're open already. I have an appointment at the Spa in ten minutes." Jimmy's mother shoved him into the room, quickly signed him in, and raced out the door.

"Would you like to play with blocks this morning?"

Jimmy nodded and raced over to the block bin. He pulled it off the shelf, dumping them all over the floor.

Olivia took a sip of tea out of her travel mug.

Rachel pushed the gate open. "Oh! It's you. I thought Irena was still here."

“She left just after I got here.”

“Oh, I was only gone five minutes. I thought cleaning the bathrooms would take more time. Jimmy is here already, huh? I thought I had at least ten more minutes.” She set a stack of construction paper down on the desk.

“His mom has an appointment at the Spa. She signed him in and was out the door before I had a chance to tell her we weren’t open yet.”

Rachel shook her head. “I got some construction paper from Nigel in the Cruise Staff Office. We were totally out of blue and pretty low on some other colors.”

“How’s Nigel?”

Rachel grinned. “He’s awesome. I haven’t seen him much this cruise, so it was nice to pop in and steal a kiss or two."

"And some construction paper."

"Yeah, that too!" She shrugged. "I mean, we did need construction paper."

Olivia picked up the stack of construction paper and carried it to the closet. She opened the door.

The arm of the pirate shirt and the wig hung out the side of the chest. Olivia lifted the lid and tucked them back in.

"Did one of the kids get in the closet?"

"Not that I know of, why?"

"I put the pirate costume away yesterday after I got changed, but it was hanging out of the chest."

Rachel shrugged.

"Hey!" Hayley pushed the gate open with her hip. She had a half eaten bagel in one hand and her coffee mug in the other. She looked at Jimmy stacking blocks and then knocking them down. "Am I late?"

"Nope. We don't open for five more minutes. His mom just brought him early."

"Figures." Hayley bit into her bagel. She looked at Olivia's mouth. "Looks much better today. I wouldn't have even noticed if I wasn't looking."

"It's still tender, but at least the swelling is down." Olivia pulled out a plastic tub filled with arts and crafts materials. "Any idea what craft we're supposed to have the kids do this morning?"

"Yes. We're supposed to make sailboats out of popsicle sticks and construction paper." Hayley showed Olivia the instructions.

"Yep, that's why I got more construction paper!"

Olivia peeled off a few sheets of colored paper, got the box of popsicle sticks out of the tub, and pulled out the bottles of white glue. "Looks like we have everything."

Parents and children lined up at the sign-in sheet. Olivia sat down in the tiny child's chair at the craft table and led the kids in making boats.

The morning went by quickly.

"Everybody, clean up!" Hayley clapped her hands. "Clean up! Everybody, clean up!"

The children raced around the room throwing blocks and toys into the bins.

"Everyone get in line at the door."

Jimmy raced to the door, shoving another little boy who was also trying to be first.

Hayley shook her head. “Nope. No shoving. Jimmy stand here.”

The rest of the kids lined up with only minimal jostling for position.

Olivia stood at the back of the line to make sure they didn’t lose any stragglers. They headed towards the Bridge. Isabella moved to the back of the line and reached up for Olivia’s hand. They moved out of the Kid’s Club and into the hallway. Olivia closed the door behind them.

The children’s excited chatter grew until they reached the passageway to the Bridge. Hayley paused and held her hand up to get the kids’ attention.”I need everyone to use quiet voices.

Many of the officers work at night and sleep during the day. We're going to be walking past their cabins so I need everyone to be quiet."

They walked down the darkened passageway Bridge door. Hayley picked up the phone on the wall outside the locked door.

"The Kid's Club is here for the Bridge tour. Yes, sir." She hung the phone up and motioned the children to stay quiet while they waited.

An officer opened the door to the Bridge and ushered their group in.

The kids chattered as they took in the commanding view of the horizon from the enormous windows lining the Bridge.

Jimmy pulled himself up on the railing trying to look out the window.

Olivia touched his shoulder. “Feet on deck, please.”

He lowered himself to the ground.

The officer stood next to Hayley. “I am 1st Officer Dimitris. Welcome to the Navigational Bridge. I hope you are enjoying your time aboard the Starlight of the Seas.”

The children buzzed with excitement as they looked around the Bridge and at the vast view of ocean surrounding the window encircled room.

A little boy pointed at the radar screens, “It’s like a spaceship!”

The kids chattered and pointed at all the electronics.

“The Bridge is the nerve center of the ship, and it is the responsibility of the captain and the officers to ensure that all the navigation, communication, and safety systems are operating efficiently. This is the area where the captain makes all important decisions regarding the ship's direction and speed. Instead of using paper charts to navigate, all of our charts have been scanned and are digital. In this monitor, you can see the chart we are using currently. The next monitor is our radar system. It shows all the traffic on the sea around the ship. We use that to see around the ship when it is dark, foggy, or during a storm."

The children crowded around the radar screen looking at all the bright colors.

The officer showed the children what the different buttons and levers did.

"The Bridge also has a variety of communication systems, including radios and satellite phones, to keep the Captain in communication with other vessels and port authorities. This is the helm of the ship. We can use this like a steering wheel to drive the ship. We can also use autopilot or program the ship so that it drives itself." The 1st officer motioned towards another officer. "Our Officer of the Watch, Christopher, makes sure that the ship stays on course and that the wind or the ocean current does not take us off course.

"Would you like to steer the ship?" The Officer pushed a small wooden box up to the helm of the ship. "Come one at a time and stand on this box."

The ship's photographer stepped forward and held up his camera.

The Navigation Officer took his hat off and put it on the first child.

One by one the children got their pictures taken.

Christopher tapped Olivia on the shoulder. “Are you new to the ship?”

“Oh no, I’ve been working on board for quite a while. I’m just helping out in the Kid’s Club this cruise.”

“Not sure how I could have missed you.”

Olivia looked down at her youth staff uniform. “Well, I’m not usually wearing this.”

“If anyone can pull off this look, it is you.” He took a step towards her.

“Oh. Um, thanks.” Olivia stepped back and looked for Hayley and Rachel. They were both helping the kids get their pictures taken.

“You miss having some adult company being with all the little kids all day?”

Christopher leaned back against the desk. "Em always enjoyed having some fun after work."

"Emerald?" Olivia asked. "Do you know Emerald?"

Christopher shrugged and smirked, "I guess you could say that."

Hayley called to Olivia, "Ready?"

Olivia held up one finger. "I'll be right behind you all."

She turned towards Christopher. "When was the last time you saw Emerald?"

Christopher crossed his arms. "What is it to you?"

"She didn't show up to work this cruise. I'm trying to track her down."

"Can't help you." He nodded towards the line of children streaming out of the

Bridge. "Looks like you need to catch up to your group."

The curtains whooshed shut in front of Olivia and Hayley.

Olivia sighed and sank to the stage floor. “We made it. Just barely, but we made it.”

“It’s been a heck of a cruise. I’ll be so relieved when this week is over and we can just perform our shows instead of spending all day wrangling kids and then performing two shows.” Hayley sat down next to her.

Tristan scooted between the proscenium wall and the curtain. “Oh! You’re still here! I was heading back to the dressing room to tell you, splendid show.”

“No thanks to you.” Hayley glared at him.

“What do you mean by that?” Tristan handed his microphone to Fernando.

“We’re exhausted. Working in the Kid’s Club and doing our shows on top of it is too much. I can’t wait for this week to be over.” Hayley’s eyes narrowed. “You have a replacement Youth Counselor coming on board next cruise, don’t you?”

Tristan rolled his eyes and pulled his white cuffs down from the sleeves of his blue uniform jacket. “I told you that Home Office was sending someone.”

“Good.”

"I really appreciate you helping me out this cruise. It would have been a bloody disaster otherwise." Tristan looked at his watch. "Nigel is hosting the game show for me tonight. Can I take you two out for a drink to thank you for everything you've done?"

Olivia shook her head and dragged herself to her feet. "I still have to tear down all the illusions and pack everything up. I won't be done for at least three more hours. If I'm going to get any sleep before I have to be up for the river rafting tour in the morning, I need to get moving. You go ahead, Hayley."

"No, I'll help you tear down."

"You've been killing yourself doing the production show and my show on top of youth staff. You haven't had a break. I'll take care of this."

"Are you sure?"

"I'm positive."

The stage curtain opened to a nearly empty Theatre.

Nell and Nigel walked through the aisles picking up dropped programs and things passengers had left behind.

Nigel picked up a green sweater he'd found, and tossed it over the handrail along the aisle.

Nell grabbed the sweater. "I'll take this to Lost and Found. I know you have to get going."

"Thanks!" Nigel handed her the sweater. "Off to pretend I'm a game show host!"

Nell tucked the sweater under her arm.

"Thanks for handling it tonight, Nigel." Tristan waved.

"Might as well. I didn't have anything else to do since Rachel has babysitting in the Kid's Club tonight."

Hayley nudged Tristan in the ribs. "See?"

"Yes, ma'am. But for tonight, can I just take you out for a drink or two and not talk about the Kid's Club?"

Hayley considered. "No."

Olivia shook her head. "Hayley, you are acting like a twit! Why are you giving Tristan such a hard time?"

Hayley glared at Olivia. "Mind your beeswax, sis."

"Thanks for trying." Tristan winked at Olivia. "I'll get some of that chocolate cake you like."

"No fair." Hayley bit her lip and sighed. "You know my weakness."

Tristan pulled Hayley into his arms and kissed the top of her head. "All is fair in love and war, my dear."

Hayley pulled back. She looked into his blue eyes and pressed her lips tightly together.

Tristan grinned and kissed her again. He raised an eyebrow. "Are you wearing your show dress out tonight? Not that I object. You look divine, but since it isn't formal night, your red sequin gown might be a little fancy."

"I'll be in my street clothes in two minutes."

Hayley changed quickly, and they headed up to the Crow's Nest.

Nell slid the window open in the Light and Sound Booth and stuck her head out. “Do you want me to shut the house lights off when I head out?”

“Sure.” Olivia shielded her eyes with her hand. “Hey, Nell. Are you going to be here for a few more minutes?”

“Yes. I am going to set up for karaoke tonight so I don’t have to do it in the morning.”

“They are doing karaoke in the Theatre? Don’t they usually have that in the Disco?”

“There is a private party in the Disco tomorrow so we moved karaoke in here.”

“Okay. Let me get changed out of my costume. I need to ask you something about Emerald. Okay?”

“Sure.” Nell slid the glass shut.

Olivia put away her linking rings and headed to the dressing room to get changed into leggings and a t-shirt.

"Hey, baby!"

"Hey, Chico. You were a good boy during the show tonight."

"Mmm. Treat?"

"Why not. You earned it." Olivia reached into her pocket and pulled out an almond. "Here you go."

Chico grabbed the almond with his foot and dug into the shell, tearing little bits off and dropping them to the floor.

"Careful there buddy." Olivia picked up the shell. "Do you want to hang with me while I take down the tricks, or do you want to go back to our cabin?"

Chico wiggled his wings and flew to Olivia's shoulder.

"Hang with me?" Olivia kissed his yellow head. "Good. I've missed you this week. Are you going to be my helper?"

"Oh, boy!" Chico danced back and forth on her shoulder. "What are you, what are you, what are you doing?"

Olivia carried him out on stage.

The auditorium was dark.

"Nell?"

The room was quiet.

"Nell? Are you here?" Olivia walked out onto the apron of the stage. "She said she was going to be here when I got changed."

"Uh oh."

"Uh oh is right, Chico." Olivia walked backstage and closed the curtains so no one would see her tearing down the illusions if they came into the Theatre "I'll have to come to karaoke in the morning and talk to her then."

"La, la la!"

"You are a good singer, but I don't think they let birds sing at karaoke. Sorry, buddy."

"La....." Chico lowered the note an octave.

She pulled the sub trunk out from the wings.

"Ugh." The trunk dragged across the floor. She braced herself and pulled again. "What the heck is wrong with this thing?"

Olivia put Chico on his ring stand and turned back to the trunk.

She lifted the lid and then closed it again. She checked the castors. "Ah ha! This one was locked." Olivia unlocked the wheel and pulled the trunk the rest of the way onstage. She packed up her props and stashed them in the trunk.

She picked Chico back up and carried him around as she packed up.

Olivia yawned. She flipped the levitation onto its side. “Here. Help me unscrew the bolts, okay?”

“Okay!” Chico scooted along the edge of the trick and spun the nuts until they fell to the floor. “Uh, oh!”

“Good boy!” Olivia scooped them up and stuck them in her pocket. “You’re a good helper.”

Chico pulled the bolts out of the holes and dropped them to the floor. “Uh, oh! Ha! Ha! Ha!”

“You like that, huh?”

They worked away at taking the rest of the illusions down.

Chico's beak hinged open and his little dark tongue wiggled as he yawned. He fluffed up his feathers and balanced on one foot.

"My little guy getting tired?" Olivia yawned. "Me, too."

She looked around the stage. "Looks like we did it. Ready to go to bed?"

"Night, night?"

"Yes, night, night." Olivia looked at her watch and yawned again. "Although it is already morning."

Chico climbed up on Olivia's shoulder and tucked himself into her blond hair. He croaked in a deep voice. "Good night."

"I get the idea. I'm ready for bed, too. Let's head out, buddy." Olivia picked up his travel cage. "Do you want to go in your travel cage or do you want to ride on my shoulder? We're probably the only souls up at this hour."

Chico tucked himself further into Olivia's hair.

"Shoulder it is, then." Olivia flicked off the work lights and climbed down the stairs into the auditorium. She carefully made her way up the darkened aisle, holding Chico's travel cage out in front of her.

Olivia paused as she yawned again.

"Night, night."

"I'm trying." She turned and kissed his green, feathered tummy. "I'm pretty tired."

Chico's cage banged against the metal edge of one of the Theatre seats.

Chico startled. "Whoa, Nelly!"

He flew off of Olivia's shoulder and landed on the floor in front of her with a thud. "Uh, oh! Oh, no!"

"Chico. Hold on. I'm coming to get you." Olivia put the cage down on the floor.

Chico ran up the aisle to the doors of the Theatre. "Hellooo!" He called out.

"Stop." Olivia jogged up the aisle towards him.

"Hello!" Chico's tail wagged back and forth, and he ran. "Uh, oh!"

Olivia caught up to him and reached down to scoop him up.

Chico darted down a row of seats.

"Dude! I'm tired. I don't want to play chase." Olivia slid into the row and scooted between the rows of seats.

Chico reached the end of the row and turned left.

Olivia exhaled. “Chico. I really don’t have it in me to play hide and go seek.”

“Uh, oh!” Chico shrieked. “Oh, no!”

Olivia reached the end of the row.

Chico stood in the aisle a few rows up in front of a woman’s foot.

A woman lay on the ground, just her leg stuck out of the row.

“Emerald?” Olivia took a step towards the person.

“Oh, no!” Chico waddled down the aisle towards Olivia.

Olivia picked him up. “It isn’t funny, Emerald. Get up. Alex thought I was crazy seeing you before.”

Chico ran up her arm, onto her shoulder, and burrowed into her hair. He shouted into her ear. “I’m a good, good boy!”

"It's okay, Chico. You didn't do anything wrong."

"Emerald. Seriously. It isn't funny." The groan of the engines echoed in her ears in the empty, dimly lit space. Shivers raced down her spine.

"Come on. Get up."

She took another step.

She reached the woman. "No!"

Nell lay sprawled on the floor between the rows of seats, a green sweater clutched in her hand. Her usual neat bob was splayed out on the floor. Her blank eyes stared up at the ceiling.

She was dead.

"Liam, I need to use a phone. It's an emergency."

"We're not supposed to let anyone use the Purser phone. How can I help you?"

Olivia leaned against the Purser Desk. "Fine, then you call. Dial Alex's cabin and then hand me the phone. I need to talk to him immediately."

Liam shook his head. "I don't have authorization to do that."

"Uh, oh!" Chico mumbled.

Olivia reached over the desk and grabbed the phone.

Liam reached for the phone.

Olivia put her hand up. “Don’t worry. I’ll take full responsibility.” She punched in Alex’s number.

His voice was deep and raspy from sleep. “Ballas.”

“Alex, it’s me. Olivia.”

“Yeah?”

“Nell is dead. I found her body in the Theatre.”

“It’s three in the morning, Liv. Did you have another dream?”

“It’s not a dream! I’m wide awake.” Olivia smacked her hand on the desk.

“Oh, boy!” Chico squawked.

Olivia shushed him and lowered her voice. “I didn’t imagine seeing a body the other night, and I'm not imagining it now."

"Where are you now?" Alex sighed. His mattress squeaked as he got up.

"With Liam at the Purser's Desk."

"Stay there. I'll be there in one minute."

"No, I'll meet you in the Theatre. I don't want Nell's body to go missing like Emerald's did."

"Stay with Liam." Alex slammed the phone down.

Olivia glared at the handset. She handed it back to Liam. "Tell Alex I'm in the Theatre."

"You found a body?"

Olivia ignored him as she raced back to the Theatre.

She pushed the door open and scanned the darkened auditorium. Nothing had changed.

Nell's foot still stuck out of the row of seats.

Olivia breathed a sigh of relief. "Alex would think I was bananas if she was missing."

"Bananas!"

"Not the time, dude."

She made her way along the back wall and into the dark booth. She bolted the door behind her and threw up the house lights. "That's better."

The Sound and Light Booth was dark and stuffy. She slid the glass window overlooking the auditorium open a couple of inches to get some fresh air.

The hair on the back of her neck stood up as the window slid closed.

Olivia backed up away from the window.

The glass slid open again.

The window glass was moving with the motion of the ship.

She took a deep breath.

Olivia slid it shut and bolted it.

She stood next to the Follow Spot and looked out the window over the rows of seats in the auditorium waiting for Alex.

Chico scooted out of her hair and walked down her arm.

Olivia brought him up to her chest and cuddled him next to her. Her hand shook as she rubbed his yellow cheek feathers.

Alex threw open the door to the Theatre. “Olivia?”

Olivia unbolted the door to the booth and threw it open.

Alex jerked towards the opening door of the sound booth and raised his arm, bracing himself for an attack. As her figure emerged, he lunged forward.

Olivia shrieked and jumped back.

Alex froze. “Son of a…!” His hand shot to his chest, his heartbeat pounding under the palm of his hand.

Chico yelped. “Son of a….!”

Olivia shushed him.

Chico mumbled to himself, scooted up Olivia’s arm and burrowed in her hair.

“You. Do. Not.” Alex’s dark eyes bored into Olivia's blue ones. “Jump out at someone after telling them you found a dead body.”

“Sorry, I didn’t mean to scare you.” Olivia raised her hands, palm out. “I wasn’t thinking.”

Alex took a deep breath. He shook his head. “Where is she?”

Olivia led him over. “Here.”

Alex knelt down next to the body. He felt for a pulse.

His head dropped.

"She's gone." He stood up. Alex pulled his radio off of his belt. He radioed Victor and filled him in. "We need the entire team here."

Within a minute, Victor pushed open the door to the Theatre. The other security staff piled in behind him.

Alex filled Victor in on what he knew so far and then led Olivia to the lobby. He sat her down on a bench by the elevator and pulled a small notebook out of his pocket. "Tell me everything you know about Nell and what happened tonight. Had you seen her earlier this evening?"

"Yes. Nell and Nigel, were picking up the trash left by the passengers in the auditorium after my last show tonight.

Tristan had asked Nigel to host the game show tonight so he could take Haley out. Nell was setting up for karaoke in the morning when I went backstage to get changed. She said she was going to be around for a while. When I came out after I got changed, I didn't see her. I just assumed she had finished and couldn’t wait for me because she had to be at her next event.”

Alex's pen scratched in his notebook. “Wait for you?”

“I had a couple of things I wanted to ask her about.”

“What did you want to ask her?”

"Nell was Emerald's roommate."

“Yes. I interviewed her after Emerald disappeared.” Alex's eyes started towards the Theatre door as his staff rushed in and out.

"I talked to Nell the other day about Emerald. She didn't seem overly concerned Emerald was missing. I didn't get the impression that she liked her much." Olivia shifted on the bench. She pushed her hand into Chico's breast and lifted him off of her shoulder. "She told me that Emerald had been bringing strange men into their cabin at night. I don't blame her for being annoyed at that. I'm so grateful my only roomie is Chico."

Alex jotted down what she had told him. "If Emerald was having men spend the night, I need to look into who those men were and if any of them know what happened to her. Did she tell you who any of these men were?"

Olivia shook her head. She cuddled Chico to her chest, putting him under his wing. “Here’s the thing. I ran into Joseph last night. He is their cabin steward, too. He said that Emerald wasn’t the roommate who had men staying over.”

“How would Joseph know that?”

“Our cabin stewards are in our cabins every day. They probably know more about us than we would expect.”

“True. I always interview the cabin stewards when there is an incident.”

“I’ll ask around and see if any of the girls on staff have any idea who was spending the night in Nell and Emerald’s cabin.”

Alex's cheeks flushed. “Absolutely not. Stay out of this, Olivia. One woman is missing and another is dead. I do not want you asking anyone any questions about Emerald or Nell. Understood?"

“Alex. I know a lot of the women who work in the cruise staff department.

They are more likely to tell me what they know than to talk to you."

"Olivia. It isn't safe."

Olivia stood up. "I won't question any men that stayed with Emerald overnight. I think I can get more out of other women than you."

"No. We're not even going to discuss this. I want you to drop any ideas about questioning anyone. I'm going to have one of my team take you to your cabin."

Olivia turned toward the crew door. "I don't need anyone to babysit me, Alex."

"Olivia. It is my responsibility to make sure nothing happens to you, or anyone else. I need to know you will be safe. Please."

"Why would I be safer with one of the men on your team? One of them might be the killer?"

"That's ridiculous, Liv. I know my men. None of them would do a thing like this. Trust me."

"Why would I trust you?" Olivia snapped.

"Ah! Ah! Ah!" Chico lifted his wings out from his body and rocked back and forth. His eyes flashing.

"It's okay, Chico." Olivia rubbed his back, calming him.

Alex rubbed his hand down his face. "What have I ever done to make you not trust me?"

Olivia's voice quavered. "It's not you."

"I'm not Peter. Stop putting what he did to you on me." Alex tipped her chin up. His thumb grazed the small bandage on her mouth. He kissed his finger and then touched it to the bandage. "I care about you. I am not going to hurt you."

"Good boy." Chico looked from Alex to Olivia and back to Alex. "Good, good, boy."

Victor leaned out of the Theatre door and gestured to Alex.

Alex held his finger up. "One second."

"Look. All of my attention needs to be on figuring out who did this to Nell and finding Emerald." Alex cupped Olivia's cheek with his hand. "I need to know you are safe so I can do my job."

"Victor, take Ms. Morgan to her cabin."

"Hey!" Chico bobbed his head up and down.

"Ms. Morgan and Chico."

"Yes, sir."

Olivia's knees stuck up to her chest as she sat in the tiny chair.

Jimmy scooted his chair back from the table and pointed at her. "You're too big."

"Thanks." Olivia handed him a paintbrush. "I hadn't noticed."

Jimmy grabbed the paintbrush out of her hands, stuck it in the blue paint, and covered the bottom half of his piece of paper with blue swirls of paint.

"Are you going to paint our boat?" Olivia asked.

Jimmy dipped his paintbrush back in the blue paint and swirled the paint brush around. "Nope!"

He covered the rest of the paper with blue paint. "I'm going to paint airplanes in the sky."

"Do you like airplanes?" Olivia picked up the artwork the other children had left scattered across the table.

"I'm going to be a pilot when I grow up. I fly planes in my video game I play at home."

"Would you like to be a cruise ship captain?"

Jimmy thought for a second. "Cruise ships don't fly."

"That is true."

"Does your bird fly?"

Olivia smiled. "He does! When I first adopted him, his feathers weren't in very good shape. They are healthy now, but he really likes to eat snacks, and that makes it a little hard for him to fly very far."

"I like snacks, too." Jimmy stopped painting. "Does that mean I won't be able to fly an airplane?"

Olivia shook her head. "Pilots eat snacks. You'll be fine! It is just harder for a bird to fly if they are heavier. I try to give him lots of exercise so he stays healthy and strong."

"Like this?" Jimmy stood up and put his arms out like wings. He made an engine noise with his mouth and zoomed in circles around the Kid's Club.

"Vroom!" Jimmy circled back towards the table. He tripped over the leg of his chair and bumped the table. A cup of red paint rocked back and forth.

"Oh no! I didn't mean it!" He jumped backwards, knocking into his chair. It tumbled backwards onto the floor.

Olivia struggled to stand up out of the low chair. She tried to grab the cup, but it was too late. The paint tipped over the side of the table and on to the carpet below.

"Son of a..." Olivia slammed her hand across her mouth before she could say anything else.

Jimmy looked at her with wide eyes. "You said a bad word."

"No, I didn't. I caught myself before I did. Jimmy, run into the bathroom and get paper towels for me, okay?

Olivia tried to scoop as much paint she could back into the cup. Paint covered her hands and dripped off the table onto her foot.

Jimmy shoved a handful of paper towels into her hand.

“Thanks.” Olivia wiped as much of the paint as she could up. She glanced at the door. “Jimmy. Your mom is here.”

“You're not going to tell, are you?” Jimmy's voice quavered.

Olivia shook her head. “No. You didn't do it on purpose. It’s okay.”

He sniffed. “I didn’t mean it.”

“I won't say anything to your mom. I promise.”

Jimmy gave her a quick hug and ran towards the door.

Olivia slid down on the floor and tried to wipe as much of the paint off the carpet as possible. It was making a bigger mess.

Hailey walked over. Her eyes bugged out. “Whoa. What happened over here?”

“Jimmy spelled the red paint.”

“Of course. Jimmy.”

“Ah, he didn’t mean it.” Olivia held out her arms. “He was just showing me what a good airplane he could be.”

“Let me call housekeeping. This is a bigger mess than we can handle.”

A few minutes later, Irena pushed her housekeeping cart into the Kids Club. She shook her head in disgust. “You didn't put paper down under the table?”

“I’m sorry, Irena. Jimmy was the only one left. I didn't think he could make that much of a mass in the couple of minutes before his mom came to get him.”

Irena filled a bucket of water in the bathroom and kneeled down on the floor. She dipped her sponge into the bucket and scrubbed as much paint as she could off of the carpet.

"I'm really sorry, Irena. I didn't mean to make such a big mess for you."

"Everyone makes a big mess that I have to clean up."

Haley called Olivia over. "Are you ready to head out? We've got the tour in an hour."

Olivia yawned. "After last night, I don't know if I have it in me to go rafting down a river. Can we cancel and go next time we're in Jamaica?"

"I've been looking forward to this all cruise. Going on this river raft tour is the only thing that has gotten me through an entire week of watching little kids."

"I know. I'm just worn out. Did you know Nell very well?"

Hayley pulled the full sign-up sheet off the pad and put it in the file drawer. “No. Not really. Tristan said he would put her in charge of an event if it needed someone who was very organized, but she could be pretty abrasive and bossy if things didn’t go her way.”

Rachel put the last clean pillowcase on the pillow and shoved it on the shelf in the closet. “I don’t want to speak ill of the dead, but Nigel told me he was sure she was trying to get him fired. He thinks she was trying to get his job. Last cruise, she redid the entire cruise staff schedule after he’d done it. It shocked him that she would do that.”

“Did he tell Tristan?”

Rachel shrugged. “I have no idea.”

Olivia leaned against the desk. “Have either of you heard any rumors about who either of them were dating?”

“Pretty sure Emerald had a boyfriend back home.” Hayley shrugged.

“Do you think Emerald went back home and there was just some kind of mess up with immigration?”

“They keep pretty thorough records. I can’t imagine them missing a crew member signing off. That could cost someone their job.”

“Do you think whoever killed Nell, killed Emerald?”

“You sure are asking a lot of questions. That’s what Tristan is worried about. They are increasing security around the ship.” Hayley slammed the desk drawer shut. “He had the audacity to tell me not to walk around the ship alone.”

"Alex said the same thing to me."

"Makes sense." Rachel shrugged.

Hayley whipped around towards Rachel. "I'm a grown woman. I don't need Tristan, or any other man telling me what to do."

Rachel held up her hands. "Hey. He just wants you to be safe."

"Sorry. I didn't mean to yell at you. I'm just not feeling like myself this cruise." Hayley glanced up at the clock above the door. "Are you guys ready?"

Rachel cocked her head. "Ready for what?"

"The river rafting tour."

"I forgot all about that." Rachel shook her head. "I'm sorry I can't go with you guys."

"Why not? This is our only day off. Can't you change your plans?" Hayley asked.

"No, I really can't. Sorry." Rachel looked at the clock and made a face. "I gotta run. Have fun."

"This is turning into a ridiculous day, isn't it? Maybe we should just cancel the excursion." Olivia's voice cracked.

"We are going to take you to your cabin, get you cleaned up and we are going to go on our river raft cruise. Do you understand me?"

Olivia shook her head. "I can clean myself up, thanks. I'm a grown woman, too. Remember? What is going on with you?"

"Sorry." Hayley picked up her bag. "I'm just on edge. That's all. I'll meet you at the gangway at 1 o'clock."

"Good." Haley headed out of the Kid's Club.

Olivia turned to Irena. “Is there anything I can help you with, Irena?”

“No. I do not need anymore help.” Irena mopped up water with her sponge and squeezed it into her bucket. “I didn’t mean to listen, but I heard you talking about Nell.”

“Yes.?”

“Rumor is that you found her.”

Olivia nodded. “Was she a friend of yours?”

Irena sneered. “No. I wouldn’t say that.”

“Oh.” Olivia shoved her hands in her pockets. “What happened?”

“Nothing.” Irena put the bucket on her cart. “Aren’t you supposed to be getting cleaned up?”

Olivia looked down at her paint covered clothes. “Right. Can you lock up when you leave, please?”

"Of course."

"Thank you." Olivia walked down the hall and turned the corner.

"Oh, no!" Alex grabbed her and pulled her into his arms. He pulled out his radio and scanned the hallway. "Who did this to you?"

Olivia pulled away from him. "Who did what to me?"

Alex lifted her hand and squinted. He rubbed the red streaks. "Paint?"

"Oh! This?" Olivia rubbed the dried red paint on her hands. "Yes, paint. Jimmy did it to me. Not on purpose, but he knocked over a cup of paint."

"You scared me." Alex put his radio back on his belt. He raked his fingers through his dark hair. He exhaled. "I thought you were bleeding."

"Sorry."

"No. It isn't your fault. I'm just on high alert."

"Still no news on Emerald or on Nell's killer?"

Alex shook his head. "You know I can't talk about that."

Olivia looked at her watch. "I need to get cleaned up.I have to be on the gangway in fifteen minutes."

"Of course." Alex took a step back. "Enjoy your time in port."

Olivia gripped the seat in front of her as the small bus whipped around the tight turn. "You're awfully quiet. Are you alright?"

Hayley pulled away from looking out the open window. "Huh?"

"I just said that you're really quiet. Are you okay?"

"I'm alright. It's beautiful, isn't it?" Hayley leaned over and peaked out the window at the river swirling next to the road.

The tour guide's voice came over the intercom. "Raise your hand if this is your first visit to my home, Jamaica."

Most of the passengers' hands raised.

"What took you so long?"

A ripple of laughter swept through the crowd.

"In Jamaica, we don't have any problems, only situations." The tour guide cupped her ear with her hand. "Can you say, 'No problem, mon.' Say it with me."

The group chorused, "No problem, mon."

"Today, we are taking you to the river to enjoy some rafting."

The bus pulled into the parking area near the bank of the river. When the woman in front of them reached down to pick up her bag, a bottle of sunblock fell out and rolled back towards Olivia. Olivia stopped it with her foot and reached down to pick it up. She leaned forward to hand it to the woman. The woman stood up and reached for her sunblock.

It was Jimmy's mother.

She glanced from Olivia to Hayley and back. A wave of recognition swept over her. "You're the magician girls."

Olivia nodded and smiled.

"You were wonderful in your show. How exciting that we have celebrities on the excursion with us. You're not going to make me disappear, are you?" She laughed at her joke and shuffled up the aisle to the door of the bus.

"Isn't it funny how much nicer she is to us now?" Hayley rolled her eyes.

"Most of the parents have been lovely, but yes, that was a change of attitude from her for sure." Olivia slid out of her seat into the aisle. "Have you ever done this excursion before?"

Hayley shook her head. "No. I was on another tour, and we went on the bridge over the river. I saw these bamboo rafts in the water and I've had my heart set on doing this tour ever since."

"I can't wait."

The aisle cleared, they made their way out of the bus and down to the group on the shore of the river.

The sun shone brightly down on the shallow river, its cool waters sparkling in the light. Lining the banks of the river were bamboo rafts, each crafted with thick bamboo poles and brightly coloured cushions. The umbrellas and tents draped in the Jamaican flag provided shade from the heat of the sun, and the passengers in the rafts floating past them enjoyed the view as the rafts cruised lazily down the river.

Olivia and Hayley stood in line, waiting to board their raft.

There were so many rafts floating in the river, you could practically cross it, walking from raft to raft.

Their group made their way onto their rafts two by two.

"Careful now, ladies. We don't want you to end up in the water." Their guide took their hands and steadied them as they climbed aboard his raft. "My name is Captain Javal, and I'll be your guide on the most beautiful river rafting trip."

Hayley and Olivia carefully made their way to the seat and settled down.

Javal walked to the front of the raft, water sloshing up between the bamboo, soaking his feet. He jammed his bamboo pole down into the water and pushed off the sandy soil below the water's surface.

A group floated past them in green and pink inner tubes.

Olivia peeked at the bank through the palm fronds and scarlet hibiscus flowers that decorated their raft. They floated past another raft. The other guide reached across and handed Olivia two flowers as they whizzed by.

Olivia tucked one bloom behind her right ear and handed the other to Hayley.

Hayley hesitated and then took the flower. She put it behind her right ear.

"Doesn't putting the flower behind your right ear mean you're single?"

Hayley scowled. “I’m not married.”

“No. You’re not married.” Olivia leaned back against the seat. “But you are in a relationship with Tristan.”

Hayley shrugged.

“Right?” Olivia turned towards Hayley.

“Let’s just enjoy the tour, okay?”

Javal walked back and forth on the raft as he guided it through the water. “This is a very safe ride. No crocodiles, no piranhas, no snakes.”

“Good to know!”

They glided through the water, passing low bungalows on each side of the river.

Olivia looked to the left and right, trying to take it all in. “Look how huge those leaves are. It is so beautiful.”

“Maybe we should get Javal to pull over.”

"Why? Are you sick?" Olivia put her hand on Hayley's knee.

"No." Hayley looked at a palm stretched out above the river as they drifted underneath. "Just thinking it would be so peaceful to live here. We could get a little cottage along the river and watch the people sail by."

"It would bore you in less than a week. What is going on? You are not acting like yourself. You've been crabby all cruise."

Another raft coasted by them. Javal stuck his pole into the water and guided them away from the other raft.

"I'm not crabby."

Olivia raised her eyebrows and looked at Hayley.

Hayley rolled her eyebrows. "Fine. I'm crabby."

"Are you mad at me? Do you not want to do the magic show with me anymore?" Olivia shifted on the low bamboo seat. "It might not even be an issue in a few weeks. My contract hasn't been renewed."

Hayley leaned into Olivia. "It isn't you! I love doing the shows with you. And I am sure that your contract will be renewed. Absolutely sure. Tristan is thrilled with your passenger ratings."

"Our passenger ratings."

"Ah, you could replace me with any of the dancers. It's you that makes the show, Livy." Hayley shrugged. "Well, you and Chico."

"Yes, Chico is the star, for sure. Good to hear that Tristan is happy. I thought they might be just keeping me on to the end of this contract so they didn't have to pay to ship out a new magic act."

"Absolutely not. Tristan was telling me he gets more comments about Chico than any of the other headliner acts. That bird is the real magic in your show."

"So if it isn't me, or the magic show, what is wrong? You are not acting like yourself."

Hayley leaned back and looked up at the branches whizzing overhead.

"I'm feeling claustrophobic."

"Outside?"

"No, in my life. When Tristan asked me to work in the Kid's Club, I felt trapped." Hayley raked her fingers through the waves of copper hair. "It was just supposed to be a shipboard fling. I don't want him expecting anything from me."

"He asked Rachel and me, too."

"I know. It wasn't him asking. It was how I felt when he asked." She rubbed her face. "I felt like I couldn't say no because we're in a relationship. That is way more serious than anything I want in my life right now. I want to be free. Travel the world and not be responsible to anyone."

"You could have said no."

"I could have. But I didn't." Hayley sighed. "That's why I'm crabby. I didn't want to let him down."

"You're a good person."

"It's more than that, Liv. I have feelings for him." Hayley bit her lip. "Uncomfortable feelings."

Olivia's eyes narrowed. "Feelings? Are you in love with him?"

"I hope not. I better not be." Hayley's knee bounced up and down. "In a few months, one of us will get a contract on another ship. We'll say goodbye, 'see you the next time our ships are both in the same port' and that will be that."

"You're rocking the raft." Olivia put her hand on Hayley's knee. "What if, instead of that happening, you make sure you take contracts on the same ships? What if you travel the world together?"

"He wouldn't want that. People don't get jobs on ships to be tied to other people. This is not the life for finding long-term partners."

"You don't know that."

"Girl, you won't even go on a date with Alex, and that man is totally smitten with you."

"I don't think you can have an opinion on falling in love at sea."

"Falling in love?"

"You know what I mean."

"Are you in love with Tristan?"

"If I am, I'm just going to have to get over it." Hayley leaned over and dropped her fingers into the water. "I want adventures. Not a serious commitment."

Javal slowed the raft as a person on a rope swing flew across the river in front of them. He guided the raft to the edge of the river. "You want to swing across the river?"

Olivia's eyes lit up. She looked at Hayley. "Do you want to?"

Hayley shook her head. "Nope. I am not jumping off that thing."

"You're not jumping off of it, you're swinging off it on a rope." Olivia climbed up the steps and held onto the edge of the tree. "Besides, even if you fell, you would land in the water."

Hayley crossed her arms. "You know how I feel about heights."

"You travel the world by yourself, but you won't swing on a tire over a river?" Olivia grabbed the thick stick at the end of the rope swing. “It’s not even that high up.”

“It’s high enough.” Hayley took a step back. “I’ll watch you have fun.”

“Ah, come on. Get out of your comfort zone. Be adventurous. Isn’t that what you just told me you wanted?”

“I didn’t mean adventures where you might risk your life. I just want you to have a drink with a handsome man and enjoy yourself a little.”

Olivia held onto the tree with one hand and leaned out over the ground towards Hayley. “So if I agree to have a drink with Alex, will you swing?”

“That seems like a win-win for you, with nothing in it for me.” Hayley wagged her finger. “And hold on with two hands. You’re making my stomach flip.”

"I guess you really don't want me to have a drink with Alex that badly then." Olivia held the rope to her chest and wrapped a leg around it. She looked both ways to make sure there weren't any rafts coming and let go of the tree and flew off the small platform over the water. She leaned back as she swung. Her long blond hair swished through the water. A giggle burbled up in her chest. She let go of the rope and dropped into the water.

Olivia popped up out of the water and shook the water out of her hair. She made her way back up onto the bank of the river.

"It's fun. Come on, try it with me?" She reached for Hayley's hand.

Hayley looked up at the platform. "Can't we have fun on the ground?"

"If you can do the levitation, you can do this."

"Can and want are two different things."

A little girl of about 7 raced up to the steps and climbed up on the platform. She grabbed the rope swing and flew out over the water. She swung back and forth and landed in the water.

Olivia looked at Hayley and grinned.

"Fine." Hayley rolled her eyes and sighed. She took a deep breath and climbed the steps. Hayley reached the platform and hauled the rope back to the platform. She glared down at Olivia. "If I die, it's all your fault."

She gripped the rope close to her chest, wrapped her legs around the rope, and closed her eyes. She took a deep breath and slid off the platform.

Her copper hair glowed in the sun and she swung back and forth. She rode the swing until it slowed and then slid off of it into the water. She walked out of the water, dripping on the muddy bank. "There. Are you happy?"

Olivia nodded. "I sure am. It was fun, wasn't it?"

"It wasn't awful." Hayley grabbed her coverup and pulled it on over her head. "So, where are you and Alex going to have your drink?"

"Wait a minute," Olivia's eyes narrowed, "You didn't swing when I made that offer."

"Was there a deadline?" Hayley pretended to look at her watch. "I never heard you rescind your offer."

Olivia opened her mouth and then shut it. “Were you just pretending to be scared?”

Hayley shrugged. “Javal is calling us back to the raft.”

Olivia bent down and picked up a pillow off of the mat. She turned towards Rachel and Hayley and held it up. “Did we leave this out when we left this morning?”

“No. I don’t think so.”

“Then why is there a pillow and mat on the floor?”

Rachel shrugged. “Maybe one of the kids came in for a nap?”

"Goodness, do you think a parent dropped their kid off not knowing we were closed?" Olivia's eyes widened. "Jimmy's mom was on the rafting tour. Do you think she left Jimmy here by himself?"

Rachel shook her head. "No. I'm sure she didn't."

"How can you be sure?"

Rachel grabbed the mat and folded it up. "I'm sure she wouldn't do that." She took the pillow and blanket from Olivia and shoved it into the closet.

One of the parents dropped off their child on their way to dinner.

"Enjoy your dinner!" Hayley signed them in.

The little girl ran into the Kid's Club and grabbed Olivia's hand. "I have to go potty."

"No problem. Follow me." Olivia led her to the bathroom at the back of the room. She held the bathroom door open for the little girl.

A red and white striped shirt lay on the bathroom floor. "Hold on." Olivia bent down and grabbed it off the floor.

The little girl went into the bathroom and shut the door. After she was done, Olivia took the shirt to Hayley and Rachel. "Did either of you leave one of your youth staff shirts on the floor of the bathroom by accident?"

Neither of them had.

"Very strange." Olivia dropped the shirt into the laundry bag with the dirty pillowcases and sat behind the sign in desk as the children arrived for the evening.

Jimmy burst into the Kid's Club. "Hi Miss Rachel. I had my dinner. What did you eat for your dinner?" He grabbed Rachel's hand and swung back and forth. Rachel led him to the play area.

Jimmy's mom wrote his name on the sign in sheet. She looked up at Olivia and recognition washed over her face. "Wait. You're the girl magician."

"Yes."

His mom scanned the Kid's Club. "And you work here, too?"

"Just helping out this cruise."

Jimmy's mom scoffed. "I thought the ship had professional entertainers."

"I am a professional entertainer. The cruise director just asked me to help out in the Kid's Club this cruise."

"If you say so." She tossed the pen down on the desk and walked out.

Hayley leaned against the wall next to the desk. "Such a lovely woman."

"Seriously." Olivia yawned. "I'll be glad when this cruise is over. I need a nap."

Shrieks rang out from the group of kids when Rachel pulled out a bin of toys. "Well, that woke me up."

Olivia grabbed the evening Kid's Club schedule and looked up at the clock above the door. "Only a couple of days left. We can do it."

Isabella ran over and handed her a picture she'd drawn.

"Thank you! Is that Chico?"

Isabella nodded. "Birdy!"

"Yes, he's a birdy. I love your picture. I am going to hang it up in my cabin where Chico can see it."

Isabella grinned and ran off to play with the other children.

Olivia walked over to the desk and tucked the drawing under the sign-in book.

A flash of white at the gate drew her attention. Her face lit up when she recognized Alex standing in the doorway. She tugged on her red and white striped shirt and tucked it into her white shorts.

Her smile faded at the expression on Alex's face.

He looked in the Kid's Club at the group of children on the floor playing. "Can you get away for a minute?"

Olivia signaled to Rachel and Hayley that she needed to step out for a minute.

Hayley's eyebrows raised when she saw Alex at the door. She gave Olivia a thumbs up. "Take all the time you need."

"I'll be back in five minutes."

"Seriously, we have everything under control. Take as long as you need."

Olivia walked out into the hallway and shut the gate behind her. "What's wrong?"

"I only have a minute." Alex's eyes darted around nervously. He pulled Olivia over to a bench across from the elevator and sat down next to her. "I shouldn't be here telling you this."

"Alex, you're scaring me. What's wrong?"

The circles under his eyes were so dark they looked like bruises. He rested his elbows on his thighs and his head drooped. "This isn't public knowledge yet, but I had to talk to you. The coast guard found Emerald."

"Oh good! Is she okay?"

"No, Liv. She isn't."

Olivia held her breath.

"She's dead. Her body got tangled up in a fisherman's net."

Olivia exhaled. "No. Oh no. I had really hoped she had gone home and the paperwork was lost."

"The back of her skull was fractured."

"From when she went overboard?"

Alex shook his head. "The autopsy suggests her skull was cracked well before she went into the water."

Alex rested his hand on her thigh.

"It was murder."

Olivia leaned back against the wall. "Two female crew members have been killed."

Alex took her hand and gave it a squeeze. "They found her on Sunday but it took this long for them to identify her."

"Wait, on Embarkation day?"

Alex nodded.

Olivia jerked forward. "Then the body I saw when I was babysitting couldn't have been Emerald."

"No one else is missing."

Olivia plucked at her top. "Who else would wear this shirt voluntarily? If it wasn't Emerald, who was it?"

Alex shrugged.

I needed to tell you as soon as I found out. I don't want you to go anywhere alone until I catch the killer. Stick close to Hayley and Rachel."

Olivia nodded. "I will."

"My staff and I are going to be increasing security and upping rounds in the evenings." Alex rubbed his face with his hands. "If you want one of us to walk you to your cabin, call."

"Come in!"

"I can't come in. My stupid key card won't work, Chico." Olivia swiped it again.

The red light flashed.

"Apparently, I need to get a new card." Olivia leaned against the door and sighed. "I'll be back."

"Who is it?"

"Chico, it's me. I'll be back in a minute."

Joseph's cart was outside a cabin at the other end of the passageway. Olivia headed towards it. She knocked on the wall outside the open door. "Joseph?"

Joseph popped out of the bathroom. "Yes, ma'am?"

Olivia held up her card. "I can't get in my cabin again."

"Oh. Of course. Give me a few minutes and I will let you in."

Olivia looked down at her watch. She held up an apple. "I need to get to the Kid's Club. I just need to give Chico his breakfast before I go to work. Can I just borrow your master key for one second?"

Joseph peered at her over the pile of towels in his hands and shook his head. "I'm not supposed to let anyone borrow it."

"I'll only be a minute. I'll let myself in, give him the apple and run the key back to you." Olivia looked at her watch. "Please? I have to get the Kid's Club open."

Joseph pulled the spiral key ring off of his wrist. A hand towel dropped to the floor. "You do not tell anyone that I let you borrow this."

Olivia picked up the towel and placed it on top of the pile. "I promise."

She slipped the key ring around her wrist and jogged down the hall to her cabin. She reached the door and looked back down the hallway.

Joseph stood next to his cart, shoving the dirty linens in the bin on his cart.

Olivia swiped the key card.

The light flashed green.

Olivia waved to Joseph and pushed the door open.

"Well, hello there."

"Hello to you too, Chico-man." Olivia held up the apple.

"Oh! Treat?!" Chico danced back and forth on his perch. "Oh, boy!"

Olivia opened his cage door and popped the apple into his dish. "That ought to keep you busy for a while. I'll try to come back at lunch."

Olivia paused at her desk. "We ran out of tape in the Kid's Club. Do I have any?" She opened the drawer and rooted around.

"Ah ha!" She shoved the roll of tape in her shorts' pocket.

"Have a good day, Chico."

Chico ignored her as he dug into his apple.

Her cabin door slammed shut behind her. She jogged down the hallway towards the cabin Joseph was cleaning.

Olivia slowed.

Nell and Emerald's cabin.

She looked down at Joseph's cart. He wasn't there.

She quickly swiped the key card.

The green light flashed.

Olivia turned the door handle and pushed the door open a couple of inches.

She looked back at Joseph's cart. Nothing.

Olivia reached into her pocket and pulled out the roll of tape. She pulled off a small piece and taped down the latch. She dragged the door shut and shoved the roll of tape in her pocket.

Joseph popped out of the cabin he was cleaning.

Blood whooshed through Olivia's ears. Her cheeks flushed. She waved to Joseph and sped up.

She pulled the key chain off her wrist. "Thank you. You are a lifesaver. I'll work on getting a new card today."

"No problem. I hope the bird liked his breakfast."

"Oh, yes! He's a happy birdy."

"Are you sure?"

Hayley waved her off. "Of course! You need to get a new card. We can handle it here. It's a quiet morning."

"Thanks."

Olivia headed to the Purser's Desk. She waited in line until Sophie was free. She pulled out her card and handed it to Sophie. "My key card isn't working. It won't open my cabin door. Any chance you can reprogram it?"

"Of course, dearie. These blasted things do this all the time." Sophie ran the card through the scanner and reprogrammed it. She handed it back to Olivia. "Should be right as rain now."

"Thank you." Olivia tucked the card in her back pocket. "Hey. Did you hear about Nell?"

"Ah, bless. I did. In her prime." Sophie sighed. She looked around the lobby and then leaned in towards Olivia. "You know I don't gossip."

Olivia nodded. "Of course."

"I heard she was dating one of the officers."

Olivia's eyebrows shot up. "Really? Do you know who?"

Sophie shook her head. "No. But I heard he was married."

A guest walked up behind Olivia in line.

"Is there anything else I can assist you with?" Sophie smiled. She looked past Olivia and smiled at the guest.

"Oh. No, that's all I needed. Thank you!"

"My pleasure. Let me know if you need anything else."

Olivia headed down the stairs to her cabin. She pulled out her key card.

She looked down the passageway. It was empty.

She shoved the card back in her pocket and casually walked down to Nell and

Emerald's cabin. She slowed in front of the door and looked behind her.

No one was there.

She gently knocked on the door and waited.

Olivia leaned against the door, and it slid open. The tape trick had worked.

The interior cabin was pitch dark with the light off. Olivia stepped inside and pulled the door closed behind her.

She shivered in the complete darkness and felt along the wall until she came to the light switch. She flicked it on and the overhead light flooded the tiny room with light.

Olivia turned the deadbolt in the door.

To her left, a door led to the tiny bathroom. Tucked between the closet and the bunk beds, a small desk gave the roommates a place to sit.

Olivia opened the bathroom door. A travel make-up bag sat on the counter and shampoo and conditioner were tucked onto the small shelf in the shower.

Olivia unzipped the makeup bag. She pulled out a tube of pink lipstick, eyeliner, mascara, and foundation. The foundation was an ivory shade.

This was Nell's makeup, not Emerald's.

Olivia put the makeup in the bag and shut the bathroom door behind her.

Voices tilted through the door as people walked down the hallway, talking. The voices got louder until they were right outside the cabin door.

Olivia held her breath as they passed by.

She exhaled as the voices got quieter. She heard a cabin door slam shut, and the hallway was quiet again.

Olivia opened the narrow closet door.

It was empty except for a lifejacket tucked up on the top shelf.

It had to be Emerald's.

Olivia opened the other closet door.

A neat row of garments hung on hangers. Each clothes hanger was an inch from the next. Nell's cruise staff uniforms hung on the right of the closet and her civilian clothes hung on the left side. A pair of sneakers, sandals, and nude pumps lined the bottom shelf.

Olivia lowered herself into the chair and pulled out a desk drawer. A couple of pens and a pink and a yellow highlighter rolled across a stack of daily schedules when Olivia pulled open the drawer.

Olivia pulled out the top schedule and glanced at the notes scrawled in the margins and the highlighted sections.

Olivia put the schedules on top of the desk. She opened up the rest of the drawers. She found hair spray, a hair dryer, a bottle of cologne, socks, and underwear. Olivia pulled the lid off of the cologne and breathed in the warm spicy scent of bay rum. She put the lid back on the bottle and put everything back inside the desk drawers.

The thin white sheets folded over the top edge of the tan wool blankets. The privacy curtains were open, tucked back at the head of the bed.

Olivia climbed the stepladder and climbed up on the top bunk. The walls were empty. She fished her hand between the mattress and the bed frame, but found nothing.

She climbed down the ladder and ducked under the top bunk. Olivia laid on her stomach and felt around the mattress. She pulled out a tube of lip balm.

She slithered out of the bed and then froze.

On the underside of the top bunk, someone had taped up a photo.

Olivia reached up and pulled the photograph off the upper bunk.

Olivia grabbed the picture and the stack of schedules and headed to the door.

She paused before leaving and opened the closet door again. One by one, she reached into the pockets of

Nell's clothes. She found a receipt for smoothies from a restaurant in St. Thomas and a pen.

Olivia pulled out Nell's blue cruise staff uniform jacket and reached into the pockets. Nothing. She reached into the breast pocket of the jacket.

She pulled out a key card on a red spiral wrist band key ring.

It wasn't Nell's ID.

Irena's picture was in the top right corner.

A door slammed in the hallway and chattering passengers passed by the door of Nell's cabin.

Olivia held her breath.

She gripped the papers to her chest.

As soon as the hallway was quiet again, she turned off the cabin light and slowly turned the door handle. She carefully pulled the door open a couple of inches and waited.

It was quiet.

She pulled the door open further and peeked out.

The hallway was empty.

Olivia carefully shut the door behind her and hurried to her cabin.

She swiped her key card.

The light flashed green.

Olivia pushed open the door.

"Well, hello there!"

Olivia shut her door and leaned against it. She clasped the daily schedules to her chest, took a deep breath, and slowly let it out. "Hello, Chico."

"What are you? What are you? What are you doing?" Chico pitched each phrase up a scale. Then he lowered his voice. "Bad, bad, bad."

"I'm not bad! I didn't do anything wrong."

"Bad bird!"

"Oh. You're not bad, either."

Chico wiggled his wings, asking to be picked up.

Olivia unlatched his cage and lifted him up. "I know you've been alone a lot this cruise. It's not your fault. I'm just really busy."

"Come. Come here."

"Do you want to come to the Kid's Club with me later?"

Chico pulled his toes out of her grip and scooted up her arm and onto her shoulder. He burrowed into her hair.

"You're going to make sure I can't leave without you, huh?"

Chico poked his head out. Olivia's blond hair covered his head.

"You look like you have a wig on, you goofy bird."

Olivia sat down at her desk and pulled out the daily schedules. She picked one up off the top of the pile.

Nell had highlighted her activities in pink.

Olivia scanned the rest of the schedule.

Nigel's activities were highlighted in yellow.

None of the other cruise staff member's activities were highlighted.

Olivia looked at the rest of the schedules. Nell had highlighted Nigel's activities on each schedule.

On one schedule, small check marks were next to Bingo and pool games. A question mark was next to Nigel's name which listed him as host for the midnight comedy show.

"Looks like Nell was keeping pretty close track of Nigel. I wonder why?"

"Uh oh!" Chico nuzzled Olivia's ear.

Olivia picked up the picture she'd found above Nell's bunk and studied it.

The silhouette of Nell's dark bob was outlined against the setting sun. A man's arm draped around Nell's shoulders, his white uniform pink from the light of the setting sun.

Nell's married boyfriend.

Olivia flipped the picture over. "O.O.W.? His initials, maybe?"

Olivia tried to make out the color and number of stripes on his epaulets. Alex would recognize the stripes and know what they meant.

Olivia rubbed her forehead. "I can't show him. Alex can't know I went into Nell's cabin."

Chico bobbed his head up and down. "Good boy, good, good boy!"

"Who is a good boy? Alex, or you?" Olivia reached up on her shoulder and tucked her hand under Chico's belly. "Up!"

Chico stepped onto her hand. "Treat!"

Olivia put him on his perch on top of his cage and handed him an almond. "That ought to keep you busy for a minute."

Chico grabbed the almond out of her hand, held it with his foot, and ripped it open with his beak. "Yum."

Olivia sat back down at her desk and picked up Irena's ID. It was on the same stretchy spiral keyring that all the cleaning staff used so they could swipe the card in the locks to open the doors of the rooms they were cleaning and it would snap back on their wrist when they opened the door.

"Why would Nell have Irena's key card, Chico?"

"Uh oh!" Chico polished off the last of the almond,"Treat?"

Olivia looked at her watch. "Not right now, buddy. If you are going to come to the Kid's Club with me, we need to get moving."

Olivia put the daily schedules and the picture in her desk drawer and closed it.

Olivia picked Chico up and put him in his travel cage.

"Let's go, buddy."

"Oh, boy!"

"Does he know how to count?" Jimmy bounced up and down. "I know how to count. One, two, three, four..."

"Good job." Olivia shook her head. "He doesn't know how to count yet. Maybe you can teach him."

Jimmy hopped up and down on one foot. "One, two, three, four..."

Olivia pulled out a sunflower seed and held it up.

Chico lunged for the seed.

Olivia pulled her hand back and wagged her finger. "Nope. One!" She held the seed up.

Chico eyeballed the sunflower seed. He lifted his foot and waved at Jimmy.

Olivia shook her head and held up the seed. "One."

Jimmy hopped from foot to foot. "One! One! One!"

“One!” Chico flapped his wings.

Olivia gave him the seed.

Jimmy froze. “He did it! He said one!”

“One!” Chico shouted and begged for another seed.

Olivia gave him another seed.

“One, one, one, one. ONE! What are you doing?” Chico sang the words up a scale.

Olivia shook her head. “Only when I ask, buddy boy.”

Chico turned around in a circle.

Olivia laughed. “Are you just going to do all of your tricks until you find one that might earn you a treat?”

“Treat!”

Olivia opened Chico’s travel cage. “Up.”

Chico stepped onto her hand.

“What did you think?”

“Think about what?” Rachel walked up behind Olivia.

"Sorry, I was being silly and talking to Chico like he understands what I am asking him."

"Uh oh!" Chico wiggled back and forth on Olivia's hand.

"You understand a lot, don't you, Chico?"

Isabella's mom signaled to Rachel to meet her outside the Kid's Club.

"Uh, can you take over for a minute?"

"Sure." Olivia continued the game with the children.

Rachel rushed out of the Kid's Club and returned a minute later. She avoided making eye contact with Olivia.

"Is Isabella's mom giving you trouble?"

Rachel's cheeks flushed. She shook her head, "No. She just had a question."

She studied Rachel's face. "What is going on? Are you feeling okay? You aren't acting like yourself."

Rachel shrugged. Her eyes darted around the room, but avoided looking into Olivia's. "Nothing is going on. I don't know what you mean."

Olivia reached down and touched Rachel's hand.

Rachel flinched and pulled her hand back. She picked up the Kid's Club schedule and traced the page with her finger. "Ah, excellent . It's time for a movie."

"No dinosaur movies, okay? Chico gets freaked out with dinosaurs."

"No problem! I'll make sure I don't offer the kids any movies with dinosaurs."

"Thanks." Olivia pet Chico's back. "I don't want him to scream and scare the kids."

"Or scare me!"

"True!" Olivia looked at the sign-up sheet. "Still no kids signed up for babysitting tonight. Thank goodness."

"Yeah." Rachel asked the kids which movie they wanted.

Olivia laid out mats and pillows for the remaining children and dimmed the lights.

"Good night!"

"Not yet, Chico. Movie time."

One by one, the parents came and picked up the tired children.

Jimmy's mom was the last to arrive. She signed the logbook and looked at Rachel. "Ten o'clock?"

Rachel nodded.

"Okay. See you then." She led Jimmy out of the Kid's Club.

"Don't we open at nine tomorrow?"

"Oh, yeah. I guess we do." Rachel's eyes darted to the clock above the door and back to Olivia. "Ready?"

"I've got to get Chico packed up. You go ahead. I'll close up."

"Thanks." Rachel grabbed her bag and headed out.

Olivia put away the mats and took the dirty pillow cases off the pillows and stuffed them into the dirty laundry bag. She picked up a couple of toys that had been overlooked.

"Ready to go to bed, buddy?"

"Good night," Chico said in a low, scratchy voice.

"Yes, time for bed." Olivia put him in his travel carrier and headed out of the Kid's Club.

Irena's cart was tucked into a corner near the door to the crew hallway. Olivia patted her pocket and felt Irena's ID. She looked for Irena, but couldn't find her. "She must be done for the day."

"All done. Good night!"

"Yeah, yeah. I'm getting us back to our cabin. Hold on." Olivia maneuvered Chico's carrier around the cart and through the crew door. She carried him downstairs and to their cabin.

She put his carrier down, pulled out her key card, and swiped it.

The green light flashed.

"Thank goodness." She carried Chico into her cabin and got him out of his travel carrier. "Ready for bed?"

"Good night!"

"That's what I figured." She kissed the top of his little yellow head. "I enjoyed spending the evening with you. Glad you came to the Kid's Club with me."

Olivia put him on his perch and pulled his cover over his cage.

"Good night."

"Good night, Chico."

Olivia turned on her reading light and turned off her overhead light.

She looked for her tote bag and realized she'd left it in the Kid's Club.

The book she was reading was in her tote bag.

Olivia sighed. She slipped quietly out of her cabin so as not to wake up Chico and headed up to the Kid's Club to get her book.

Olivia climbed the stairs to the Kids' Club. The crew door hit Irena's cart when Olivia pushed it open. She slid through and headed towards the Kid's Club door. She opened the door and looked behind the desk for her tote bag.

Olivia stopped in her tracks.

In the corner of the room, a shadow of a figure sprawled on the ground.

Olivia made out the red and white striped youth staff shirt on the woman.

Her breath caught and panic bubbled up in her chest from worrying that something had happened to Hayley or Rachel.

Olivia's heart raced as she approached the figure.

Olivia screamed as the person sat bolt upright.

"Irena!" Olivia clutched her chest. "What on earth are you doing in here? You scared the daylights out of me."

"I scared you? You scared me!" Irena leapt up. She pulled on her shirt, trying to cover her naked legs.

Olivia backed up. "Why are you in here? I am going to call security."

"No!" Irena shrieked. She burst into tears. "I can't lose my job. Please! Don't report me."

"Then you had better explain what is going on." Olivia laid her hand on the phone. "You have thirty seconds or I'm calling security."

Irena waved her hands. "No, no. I will tell you everything. I can't afford to lose my job. My daughter is sick. She's back home with my parents. I need to keep working to send money for her treatment."

Tears ran down Irena's cheeks. "I lost my key card. I can't get into my cabin, so I've been sleeping in here on the mats."

Olivia reached in her pocket and pulled out Irena's card. "This?"

Irena gasped. "Where did you find it?" She grabbed the card out of Olivia's hand and pulled her into a hug.

Olivia stiffened and pulled back. “Did you have anything to do with the deaths of Emerald and Nell?”

Irena’s face crumpled, and she cried harder.

She didn't deny it.

Olivia lifted the phone.

“No! Please don’t call anyone. Let me explain.” Irena grabbed the blanket off the floor and clutched it to her chest. “I had nothing to do with either of their deaths. I have been so scared that I would be next. At first, I couldn’t sleep at night, I was so worried. But I’m so tired from only catching a couple of hours of sleep a night that my exhaustion won out.”

“Why didn’t you just go to your supervisor and explain that you had lost your key card?”

"I've already gotten two warnings during this contract. If I get a third, they will send me home. If I can't pay for my daughter's medicine, she will die." Irena's bottom lip trembled. "It is a master key card. Losing it is a fireable offense all on its own."

Olivia felt a wave of pity for her, but also a sinking feeling of dread. "Tell me what happened from the beginning."

"I've been pulling extra shifts trying to make extra money. If one of the other house keeping staff wants time off, they have been giving me a little bit of cash to cover their duties. It is against regulations. On the final night of last cruise, I was working up by the pool for one of my friends. I was picking up dirty towels and dishes. When I finished, I couldn't find my key card anywhere.

I thought it might have slipped off my wrist when I was putting the towels in the dirty towel bin by the pool. I pulled them all out and went through them, but I didn't have any luck."

Irena's eyes glistened with tears as she recounted losing her ID card. "I kept hoping I would find it. I have searched this entire ship looking for it. Where did you find it? By the pool?"

"Do you clean any of the cruise staff cabins?"

"No. I'm not a cabin steward. I'm a housekeeper."

"You said you were picking up shifts for your friends. Did you take any shifts for a cabin steward?"

Irena shook her head. "Why do you ask?

Olivia tilted her head. "How did you know Nell?

"Nell? I saw her around the ship, but I didn't really know her."

"Why are you wearing a youth staff shirt? Is it Emerald's?"

Irena looked down at the striped shirt. "Oh, this? I don't know who it belonged to. I found the shirt in the pirate trunk and have been sleeping in it. Since I couldn't get into my cabin, I haven't been able to get my clothes. I only have one uniform. I've been wearing this when I have to send my uniform to be cleaned. Where did you find my card?"

Olivia hesitated. She didn't know if she could trust Irena to not tell anyone that she had been in Nell's cabin. "The night I was in here so late with that little girl, Isabella. Where did you sleep?"

"You know."

Olivia shook her head. “I don’t know. That’s why I’m asking.”

“You found me in the hall. I thought for sure you were going to report me and that was going to be the end.”

“I found you in the hall?”

“I didn’t mean to fall asleep.” Irena nodded. “I didn’t expect anyone to be around that time of night, so I just sat down for a minute. I was just going to rest, but I was so tired I fell asleep.”

“That was you?”

“Yes. I figured if I pretended to be asleep, you would think I was just a drunk passed out or something.”

“I thought you were dead.” Olivia closed her eyes. “I called Alex… the security officer, and woke him up to investigate. He thought I dreamt I had seen a body when we went upstairs and no one was there."

"I didn't mean to cause trouble for you." Irena took a deep breath. "Are you going to report me?"

Olivia shook her head. "You have your key card now, so you won't have to sleep in here anymore, right?"

"Yes. Thank you so much." Irena gathered up the mat and pillow and put them away. "I can't wait to sleep in my own bed."

Olivia shielded her eyes with her hand as the door opened and sunlight poured into the elevator. The chattering of the kids quieted as the bright sun hit them. Rachel, Hayley, and Olivia coaxed the kids out of the elevator and out onto the pool deck.

Olivia took Isabella's hand. "Everyone grab a buddy!" She led the line of kids to the mini-golf course on the opposite side of the smoke stack. The kids gasped as they spotted the colorful course.

The kids checked out the pirate-themed obstacles of various shapes and sizes.

Jimmy tugged on Olivia's shirt. "Arr matey."

The wind blew Olivia's hair in front of her eyes. She held it back with her hand. "You won't make me walk the plank, will you?"

Jimmy giggled and ran in a circle around Olivia.

Hayley handed out short plastic clubs and golf balls to the children. "Ready? Who wants to play golf?"

Olivia leaned over and showed Isabella how to hold her club. She stood up. "Just hit the ball gently. Aim for that hole down at the end."

Isabella wiggled back and forth. She swung and missed the ball. She shoved the club towards Olivia and buried her head against Olivia's leg.

"It's alright. You can try again." Olivia placed the little girl in front of her and held her hands around the club. She helped Isabella swing and connect with the ball. The ball bounced along the fake green grass and ricocheted off of a rock before it stopped near the hole. "Good job!"

Jimmy held his blue club up to his shoulder. He thrust it forward like a sword. "On guard!"

Isabella bounced up and down. Jimmy turned and almost whacked her with his club.

"Keep your club on the ground, Jimmy. You don't want anyone to get hurt." Olivia dropped a ball onto the ground.

"Here you go. See if you can get it into that hole down there."

Jimmy whacked at the ball, swinging the club up towards the sky. The golf ball shot up and out of the roped off lane for the first hole and bounced twice. The second bounce sent it over the railing, down twelve decks, and into the ocean.

"I didn't mean it!"

Olivia rubbed his back. "It's alright. It happens. Now the fish can golf. Just don't hit this one as hard, okay?" She dropped another ball down for him. "We need to keep the balls on the ground."

Isabella jumped from foot to foot. She pulled on Olivia's hand and motioned for her to come closer.

Olivia knelt down next to her.

Isabella cupped Olivia's ear and whispered, "I gotta go potty."

"Didn't you go before we left the Kid's Club?"

Isabella shrugged her shoulders and shoved her thumb into her mouth.

"Okay. Hold on. I need to let Miss Hayley and Miss Rachel know." Olivia filled them in and then led Isabella to the bathroom near the pool. She helped the little girl into the stall. The door swung open. "Turn the lock on the door."

"I'm on the potty."

Olivia grabbed the top of the door and held it closed. She rested her head against her arm. She looked down at the tile floor. Something gold sparkled between the bathroom stall and the wall.

Olivia waited for Isabella to finish and then bent down to inspect the piece of gold metal while Isabella washed her hands.

Olivia pulled on the gold metal. “Ouch!” Something stabbed her finger. Olivia wiped the pinprick of blood onto a paper towel. She wiggled the piece of metal back and forth until she could finally pull it free.

It was Emerald's name tag.

“All done.” Isabella wiped her hands on her shorts.

Olivia handed her a paper towel and then swept her up in her arms. “Let’s go, buttercup.”

Olivia carried her back to the mini-golf course and deposited her with the other children. She tapped Hayley on her shoulder.

“What’s up? Is Isabella alright?”

"Yeah, she's fine. She made it. No accidents." Olivia held up the name tag. "Look what I found in the bathroom."

Hayley shielded her eyes from the sun and read the name tag. "Emerald's? Oh, wow."

"Do you think you and Rachel can handle the kids by yourself for a bit? I want to take this to Alex."

"Of course. We're fine." Hayley looked at her watch. "It's almost lunchtime. Maybe you and Alex can discuss your find over a romantic meal."

Olivia tugged her youth staff shirt. "Sure. I'm totally dressed for romance."

Olivia raced down to Alex's office and banged on the door.

No answer.

The Purser's Desk was quiet. Olivia peaked in Sophie's office and caught her eye. “Any idea where Alex is? I need to talk to him.”

“Can’t say as I do. I can call him on his radio, though.”

Olivia hesitated, hoping she wasn’t overreacting. “Sure. Thanks.”

“No worries.” Sophie picked up her radio and made the call.

“He’s on the Bridge.”

“Thanks, Sophie. You’re the best.”

Olivia took the steps two at a time. She slowed as she reached the passageway to the bridge. She was just about to knock on the door when Alex opened.

“Are you alright? Sophie radioed me.”

Olivia nodded. “Yes, but I need to talk to you. I just need a minute.”

Alex turned towards Christopher. “I’m going to take my lunch. Congratulations. I’m thrilled for you and your missus.”

"Thank you. My fourth child. Can you believe it?"

Alex waved, and they headed out. "Do you have time for lunch? I'm starving."

"Uh, can I tell you what I found first?"

"I'm starving. Is it an emergency?" Alex held the door open for her. "Anyone in immediate peril?"

"No."

"Then let's talk while we eat."

"Sure." She picked up her pace to keep up with Alex.

"Lido Buffett?"

Olivia nodded.

They got their food and headed over to a table in the back corner.

"So, what did you want to talk about?" The corner of Alex's mouth turned up in a half smile.

Olivia pulled Emerald's name tag out of her pocket and slid it across the table to him.

He picked it up and read the name. His brow furrowed. "Emerald? Where did you get this?"

Olivia explained how she found it in the bathroom near the pool.

"You should have left it there. This is evidence." Alex pushed his plate away.

Olivia's voice rose. "I didn't know it was her name tag. I just saw the flash of metal and pulled it out. I can't do anything right as far as you're concerned, can I?"

"Sorry. I didn't mean to jump on you." Alex picked up his radio and called Victor. "Lock the women's bathroom by the pool. I'll be up in five minutes."

Alex stood up. "Thanks for bringing it to me."

Olivia pushed her chair back from the table. "I'm coming with you."

"Finish your lunch."

Olivia grabbed her sandwich and took a big bite. "There. I'm done." She stood up and crossed her arms.

"Fine. But don't touch anything."

Olivia rolled her eyes. "You do realize how many people have used this bathroom in the past week, don't you?"

Alex let out an exasperated breath. "Unfortunately, I do."

Olivia and Alex crossed the Lido Deck to the pool. Alex pushed on the bathroom door.

"Hey, it's a ladies' room."

"Oh, right." Alex's cheeks flushed. "Can you check and make sure it is empty?"

"Good thing you have me here, isn't it?" Olivia raised an eyebrow. She pushed open the door and peeked into the stalls. "All clear."

"Show me where you found her name tag."

Olivia knelt down and pointed to the narrow space between the metal support leg of the stall door and the tiled wall. "Right here."

She stood up and backed out of the way.

Victor pulled the door open and stopped short when he saw Olivia. The joyous sounds of children splashing in the pool filtered in through the open door.

"It's alright. You can come in. I'm with Alex." Olivia waved towards Alex, kneeling near the stall.

Alex examined the area. "Victor, there are a few dark curly hairs stuck in the hinge. They could belong to Emerald. We need to close off this bathroom so I can collect them and any other evidence we find. Ask the pool bartender to make a sign that the bathroom is closed and directions to another one on this deck."

"Of course, sir."

Victor came back a minute later. "Sir, when I told the bartender that the bathroom was going to be closed, he said 'again?" Apparently, at the end of the last cruise, one of the cruise staff members told him that the bathroom was out of order."

"Which cruise staff and why was it closed?"

"I'm not sure. I didn't ask." Victor taped the sign to the door. "Do you want me to go back and ask?"

"No, thank you. I'll talk to him."

Olivia followed Alex across the pool deck, dodging splashes of water from the pool.

"Don't you need to get back to the Kid's Club?"

"Hayley and Rachel have it handled." Olivia looked at her watch. "Besides, I have fifteen minutes left on my lunch break."

"Fine. Leave the questioning to me, okay?"

"Victor said that the women's restroom had been closed down recently. Do you know why?"

The bartender shrugged. "I don't know. It caused lots of problems for the cleaning staff, wet people dripping all over the floors on the way to the restroom near the buffet."

"Who closed the bathroom?" Alex rested his arm on the bar.

"It was one of the cruise staff. I don't remember her name."

"Her? It was a woman?" Olivia asked.

Alex glared at her.

"Yes, short with dark hair." The bartender dried a plastic margarita glass with his towel. He held it up to the light and then slid it into the glass holder. He put his hand at the side of his chin. "Hair like this."

"Nell." Olivia grabbed Alex's arm. "Her hair was in a bob. None of the other female cruise staff have that haircut."

Alex put his hand on hers. He lowered his voice. "Olivia."

Olivia crossed her arms.

Alex turned towards the bartender. "What happened?"

"Sure. The pool deck was really crowded that night. They had the dance party up here. That is why it was so inconvenient having the toilet closed."

"Did Nell say why it was closed?"

The bartender shook his head and then acknowledged a passenger signaling for another round. "Anything else?"

"Not right now, but maybe later."

"Of course." He walked off to make the passenger's cocktail.

Olivia tapped her fingers on the bar top. "Nell closed the bathroom and Emerald's name tag was stuck by the stall. Do you think their killer is someone who works here?" She scanned the crowd around the pool and looked back at the bartender. She leaned in close to Alex. "The bartender acted like he didn't know Nell, but do you think he was telling the truth?"

Alex gripped Olivia's forearm and led her away from the bar. "I think it isn't anything you need to worry about."

"Do you know if he is married? Sophie told me that Nell had been dating a guy and found out he was married."

"Olivia. I'm serious. Whoever killed Emerald and Nell is dangerous. Stay out of this and let me handle it."

Olivia looked at her watch. "I need to run and get to the Kid's Club."

"Good." Alex's hand touched hers. "Be careful. Okay?"

The noise of the passengers playing in the pool muted behind her.

Olivia nodded. "As long as Jimmy doesn't headbutt me in the lip again, I should be safe in the Kid's Club."

Alex rubbed his thumb across the red line next to her lip. "Almost healed up."

Olivia's breath caught, and a wave of heat flushed her cheeks. "I'd better go."

Alex's dark brown eyes held her blue ones. "Yeah. You probably should."

Olivia licked her lip and reminded herself to breathe as she walked past the pool. She looked over her shoulder.

Alex stood in the shade of the bar, watching her walk away.

"Thank goodness you're here." Hayley motioned Olivia to follow her to the desk. "Rachel didn't show up after lunch. I don't know where she is. I called her cabin, but she didn't answer."

"Do you want me to go look for her?"

Hayley shook her head. "I talked to Nigel. He's going to see if he can track her down."

"Good. With Nell and Emerald's killer on the loose, we need to make sure she is okay."

"He said he'd keep me posted. Jimmy's mom is up in arms over the picture the photographer took of him when we did the Bridge tour. Apparently, her little angel stuck out his tongue, and the photographer didn't take a second picture. She's demanding we do a reshoot."

Olivia rolled her eyes.

"Tristan told me she's related to one of the bigwigs at Home Office. I called the photographer, and he said that if we can get Jimmy up there in the next fifteen minutes, he'll do a retake." Hayley nodded towards Jimmy. "Can you take him?"

"Sure. I can do that."

"Thanks." Hayley called Jimmy over. "We're going to do a nice smile this time, right?"

Jimmy grinned.

"If you smile exactly like that, it would be perfect." Olivia took Jimmy's hand. "Ready?"

They headed up to the Bridge. Olivia knocked on the door and waited.

Christopher opened the door. His eyebrows shot up. "Back to visit so soon?"

Olivia held up Jimmy's hand. "Just here to get his picture retaken."

"The photographer called. He has been delayed, but he should be here soon."

Olivia took a step back. "We can wait outside until he gets here."

Captain Vasopoulos stood up from his chair. He caught sight of Jimmy. "Hello, young man. Would you like a tour of the Bridge? Want to sit in my chair?"

Jimmy bounced up and down. "Do I ever!"

The Captain led him over to his chair, lifted him up, and deposited him in it.

Olivia took a step towards them.

Christopher threw his arm around her shoulders and pulled her towards him. "Come look at the view from over here."

He guided her to the wing of the Bridge on the port side of the ship.

Olivia shrugged off his arm. She stood cautiously at the edge of the glass panel in the floor. She leaned over and looked down at the ocean whizzing past.

"You can stand on the glass. It will hold you." Olivia felt Christopher's breath on her neck.

Olivia took a step onto the glass. His cologne wafted over Olivia. Olivia tried to place where she had smelled it before.

"You should come up here after dark. You can't beat the view at night. Especially when the moon is full." He took a step closer to her. "I'm on duty tonight."

"Um. Thanks for the invitation. I'll keep that in mind." Olivia stepped back. Her back hit the railing in front of the plate-glass window.

The photographer knocked on the door.

"I'll be back. Stay here." Christopher went to let him in.

As soon as he left, Olivia crossed the bridge to where the Captain was showing Jimmy the radar screen.

The Captain took his hat off and plopped it on Jimmy's head. It covered his eyes. Jimmy giggled as the Captain tipped it back.

The photographer pushed a box up next to the helm and held Jimmy's hand as he climbed onto the box. He snapped a picture of Jimmy with the Captain's hat. "Since you guys are here, would you mind taking a picture with him?"

"Our pleasure." The Captain called Christopher over. "Someday, we'll be taking a picture like this with your son."

"Yes, sir."

Captain Vasopoulos looked at Olivia. He patted Christopher on the shoulder. "Did he tell you his big news?"

Olivia shook her head.

"His wife is expecting their fourth." Captain Vasopoulos smiled at Christopher. "Such a blessing."

The photographer got his last couple of shots.

Olivia held out her hand to Jimmy. "Ready to go back to the Kid's Club?"

"I'd rather stay here and drive the ship." Jimmy hopped from foot to foot.

Captain Vasopoulos took his hat off of Jimmy's head. "I think my Officer of the Watch has that covered this afternoon. We enjoyed your visit, son."

Jimmy led Olivia to the door, chattering about his time with the Captain.

Christopher stood in front of the exit. "Don't forget. I'm on duty this evening. Come back and I'll give you a special tour. Maybe we can have a late dinner."

Olivia held Jimmy in front of her. "What would your wife think?"

He shrugged and winked. "What she doesn't know...."

Olivia coaxed Jimmy through the door and down the passageway. Olivia raced towards the Kid's Club. Jimmy skipped along beside her, chattering about the Captain and the Bridge.

Olivia tried to concentrate on what Jimmy was saying, but her mind kept going back to Christopher. Other than her dislike of him, there was something tugging at her. She couldn't think with Jimmy talking.

Rachel greeted them when they got to the Kid's Club. Her cheeks were flushed red and her eyes were bloodshot.

Olivia sent Jimmy in to join the other children. "Are you alright?"

Rachel sniffed. “Sorry I wasn’t here after lunch. I just laid down for a minute and I fell asleep.”

“Are you coming down with something?” Olivia glanced at Hayley. “Hayley and I can handle the kids if you aren’t feeling well.”

A tear trickled down Rachel’s cheek. Her voice quivered. “I’m not sick.”

Olivia took Rachel by the arm and led her to the chair behind the desk. She motioned to Hayley. Hayley got the kids settled playing and came over.

“What’s wrong?” Hayley’s eyes darted from Olivia to Rachel.

Olivia shrugged and handed Rachel a tissue.

“It’s Nigel.” Rachel blotted her tears.

Hayley’s eyes narrowed. “What did he do? If he hurt you...”

Rachel shook her head. “No, he didn’t hurt me. He got a promotion.”

“That’s great news.” Hayley’s smile froze. “Wait, if he got a promotion, what is happening to Tristan?”

“Nothing.” Another tear ran down Rachel’s cheek. “Nigel is getting transferred to another ship. He’s going to be promoted to cruise director there. He told me when he came to wake me up after lunch.”

Hayley shook her head. “This is a perfect example of why there is no point in getting into a serious relationship when you work on a cruise ship.”

“Oh, no!” Olivia knelt down next to Rachel. “I’m so sorry.”

Rachel blew her nose. “I have to be happy for him, right? This is his dream.

He's worked hard for years for this promotion."

Olivia handed Rachel another tissue. "Can you go with him?"

"He didn't ask me. Besides, I have four months left in this contract." Rachel dried her eyes. "I'm sorry. I'll get myself together."

"If he asked you, would you want to go?"

"I couldn't even if I wanted to. I need to keep working. I need the money."

"You could understudy the cast on his new ship until an opening came up."

"No, I can't go months without getting paid."

"Your expenses would be pretty low living on the ship."

"No! Don't try to make it work. I don't have a choice. I have to do whatever

I can to make more money, not less." Rachel's voice trembled. "I really need extra cash."

"How much do you need?" Olivia reached into her pocket and pulled out her wallet. "If you need more than I have..."

"I can't take your money." Tears streamed down her cheeks. "Thank you for offering, but this isn't a short-term problem. My mom is having surgery. She's a real estate agent, and she's going to be out of work for months. When she doesn't work, she doesn't make money. The winter time is already a quiet season for real estate in Nags Head and now she will miss the busy spring season while she recovers."

Olivia pulled Rachel into her arms. "Oh, sweetie. I am so sorry."

Jimmy ran up and grabbed Rachel's hand. "Miss Rachel! Miss Rachel! My mom said you were going to watch me again tonight."

Rachel's eyes widened, "Uh, yeah. See you tonight." She tousled his hair and sent him back to his friends.

Olivia picked up the baby sitting sign up sheet. "I didn't see Jimmy on the list for babysitting tonight."

"He's not. I've been babysitting for Jimmy and Isabella under the table for extra money. I know it is against the rules to babysit for passengers outside of the Kid's Club, but I really needed the extra cash." Rachel swallowed and her eyes darted around the room. "I can't afford to get fired. I need to be able to help my mom with her bills."

Olivia held up the picture she'd taken from Nell's cabin. She held it close, looking for clues who the man with his arm around Nell's shoulders was. She flipped the picture over. "O. O. W. Do we know anyone with those initials, Chico?"

"Hey, baby!" Chico danced back and forth on top of his cage. He leaned forward and wiggled his wings, begging Olivia to pick him up.

"You are so goofy. You know you could just fly to me, right?" Olivia reached up and picked him up.

He ran up to her shoulder and cuddled up to her neck. "Oh, baby, baby!"

"You have babies on the brain, Chico." Olivia paused. She looked closer at the couple in the photograph. They weren't standing out on deck. The reflection on the floor behind them was the glass floor on the wing of the Bridge.

Olivia flipped the picture over. 'O.O.W.'

"Officer of the Watch. Chico. Christopher was her married boyfriend."

Chico slid off her shoulder as she shivered.

"Uh oh!"

"Sorry, buddy."

"Treat?"

Olivia put Chico on his perch and handed him an almond. "Wish me luck. I am going to have to fess up to Alex that I went into Nell's cabin."

"Oh, baby."

"You got that right."

Olivia held her breath as she knocked on Alex's office door.

"Yes?"

Olivia opened the door. "Hey."

"Oh, hey!" Alex squared the pile of papers on his desk and moved it over to the side. "What are you doing up so late? Come in. Have a seat."

Olivia perched on the edge of the chair. She looked down at the photo of Nell and Christopher.

"What's up? Are you alright?" Alex leaned forward.

"I've been better." Olivia sighed. "I have to tell you something. Please don't be mad at me. Okay?"

Alex leaned back in his seat. His sleeves pulled across his arm as he folded his arms in front of his chest. "What did you do, Liv?"

Olivia took a breath to protest and then realized that she had done something she wasn't supposed to and didn't have a leg to stand on. She shoved the photo across Alex's desk. "I found this."

Alex looked at the picture and then back at Olivia. "Found it? Isn't that Nell?"

Olivia nodded. "Nell and her married boyfriend."

Alex scratched his head. “Where did you find this? And how do you know her boyfriend is married?”

“Can we talk about where I found it later?” Olivia jabbed her finger at the Officer in the photo. “I need to tell you about him.”

“Fine. We’ll revisit where you found it later. What about him?” Alex held the photo up closer to his face and looked at his epaulets. “Christopher? The Officer of the Watch?”

Olivia nodded. “Sophie told me that Nell was dating a married man.”

“Why do you think Christopher is the man she was dating?”

“I don’t know for sure.”

Alex put down the picture. “Christopher is friendly to everyone.

Besides, he and his wife are having a baby. He's so excited about it."

Olivia pressed her lips together. "When I was up on the Bridge today, Christopher was hitting on me. His wife being pregnant hasn't stopped him from hitting on women."

"Why were you up on the Bridge?"

"It doesn't matter."

Alex's hand clenched into a fist. "He hit on you?"

"More than once." Olivia shrugged. "It happens all the time. Usually it isn't that big of a deal and when you make it clear you aren't interested, the guy backs off."

"Christopher didn't back off?" Alex raised one eyebrow. "I'll talk to him."

Olivia shoved the picture back towards Alex. "We need to ask him if he killed Emerald and Nell."

"Did he have an affair with Emerald, too?"

"I don't know, but they are both dead." Olivia shrugged. "We won't know if he was responsible until we ask him and see how he reacts."

"First of all, there is no 'we' asking anything." Alex stood up. "Victor is on his way to my office. When he gets here, send him up to the Bridge. You are to stay here. Understood?"

Olivia sunk back in her chair. "Understood."

Alex flung open his office door.

He turned and leaned back into his office. "So, when you say it happens all the time that guys hit on you.... never mind. We'll talk about that after I handle this."

Olivia's knee bounced up and down as she waited for Victor. Alex had said he would be there in just a minute. She watched the second hand travel around the face of the clock on the wall behind Alex's desk.

She picked up the picture of Nell and Christopher.

Her gut clenched, thinking of his cold eyes when she'd mentioned his wife.

Olivia leapt from her chair and peaked out Alex's door.

No sign of Victor.

Olivia crossed the lobby to the Purser's Desk.

"Sophie. If you see Victor, send him to the Bridge, asap. Okay?"

"Right. I will." Sophie held up her radio. "Should I page him?"

Olivia nodded. “Please. I’m going up to the Bridge if anyone comes looking for me.”

Olivia bounded up the steps, taking them two at a time. Her lungs burned when she breathed by the time she reached the Navigation Deck.

Olivia turned down the Officer’s Hallway. Deep voices rumbled through the door to the Bridge. Olivia tried the door handle on the door to the Bridge.

The door was locked.

She knocked on the door.

The voices rose, but she couldn’t make out what was being said.

Olivia ran down the passageway, banging on the doors of the officers’ quarters, hoping someone would answer.

Olivia heard a crash from inside the Bridge.

Her heart pounded. She slammed against the door of the Bridge, but it wouldn't budge.

"Alex!" Olivia shrieked.

She could hear the sounds of a struggle, but couldn't get the door open.

Olivia raced down the passageway and down a flight of steps. She threw open the crew door and ran out onto the deck at the bow of the ship. The wind whipped her hair behind her. As the door closed behind her, the deck plunged into darkness. The darkness of the night cloaked the cruise ship as it sailed across the open sea. The horizon stretched out in front of the ship, dark and endless.

She paused and let her eyes adjust to the darkness and then made her way to the edge of the deck where she could see into the Bridge. The only light that pierced through the darkness was that of the moon, reflecting off the shining metal of the Bridge.

The only light coming from the darkened Bridge was a faint light from the console's glowing buttons.

Olivia strained to see into the plate-glass windows of the Bridge.

The glow of lights from the navigation system's display silhouetted the shadows of two struggling figures.

"Son of a..." Olivia jumped up and down, waving her arms. No one could see her down here. She swung the door open and ran back upstairs. She banged on each cabin door as she ran back to the Bridge.

A groggy officer in his pajamas pulled open his door. “I’m not on duty until oh five hundred hours. What do you want?”

“Give me your key card!”

“No! Who are you?” he took a step back and pulled the door shut.

Olivia slammed her shoulder against the door and braced it open. “Give me your key card. Now! Alex Ballas is being held hostage in the Bridge.”

The officer grabbed his key card off his desk and pushed past Olivia. He banged on the Bridge’s door.

No one answered.

Olivia’s heart pounded at the sound of a crash on the other side of the Bridge’s door.

He scanned his key card and threw the Bridge's door open as soon as the green light flashed.

Olivia pushed past him and ran towards Alex.

Alex's arms extended as he pushed Christopher away.

Christopher gripped Alex's neck. Christopher lurched towards the panel, slamming Alex against the radar screen.

Behind Olivia, the Officer radioed for help.

Olivia's hands shook. "Alex!" She pointed at the vessel directly in front of their ship on the radar screen.

He grunted as he wrestled Christopher.

Christopher swept his foot under Alex's feet, knocking him off balance. The metal cabinets of the station clanged as Alex landed on them. He raised his foot to waist level and kicked out at Christopher, knocking him back into the Captain's chair.

Olivia circled the fighting men. She glanced at the Officer yelling into his radio. She yelled, "Get Victor. Now!"

Alex's cheeks flushed red as Christopher's fingers dug into his neck.

Olivia's eyes swept over the men.

She lurched forward, grabbing the taser off of Alex's belt. She shoved it into Christopher's neck and pushed the button. He jerked and sank to the floor.

Alex bent over, coughing and gasping for air.

Victor ran through the door and slid across the floor.

Christopher pulled himself up on the edge of the Captain's chair.

Olivia raised her foot and kicked him in the chin, knocking his head back. He landed with his back on the helm. Olivia screamed, “Victor! Cuffs.” She swiped her leg between Christopher’s back and the console, knocking him forward. She jammed her knee into his back, folding him forward and pushing his chest down onto his legs.

Victor and Alex grabbed Christopher’s arms and flipped him onto his stomach. Alex kneeled on his back, shoving his face into the ground, while Victor cuffed his hands behind his back.

Alex stumbled away from Christopher, coughing. He rubbed his neck with one hand and held his side with the other.

Alex’s chest heaved as he tried to catch his breath. “Where... did... you learn.. to do that?”

"Huh? Oh, that." Olivia watched Christopher writhing on the floor. "My uncle is a cop. He made me take self defense when I was a kid."

"Bless him."

"You'd like him."

"I'm sure I would."

"Yes, sir." Alex kept one eye on Christopher as he lay swearing on the ground. He glanced at the Captain and back at Christopher. He nodded in response to the Captain's orders. "Yes, sir."

Captain Vasopoulos climbed into his chair and crossed his arms. He studied the radar screen, barking orders to the other officers as they worked to get the ship back on course.

Alex knelt down on the floor next to Christopher's head. "Why did you kill Emerald?"

Christopher twisted trying to raise his body off of the ground. "I didn't kill her.

Alex nodded at Victor to lift Christopher off the ground. They raised him up and sat him with his back to the wall.

"Tell me more about Nell." Alex's voice was low and reserved. "Why did you kill her?"

Christopher spat blood on the group and glared at Alex. "It was just a brief fling. You know."

"I'm sorry. I don't know. Explain."

"She got serious. She actually thought I was going to leave my wife for her." Christopher scoffed. "When she found out that my wife and I were going to have a baby, she went out of control.

She threatened to tell my wife about our fling. Can you believe that?"

"If you didn't want your wife to know you were cheating, maybe you shouldn't have cheated."

"Come on." Christopher rolled his eyes.

"You killed her because she told your wife?"

"No!" Christopher raised his chin. A trickle of blood dripped out of his mouth and down his chin. "She thought she was clever. That she'd make me jealous."

Christopher's eyes glazed over and he looked off into space. "Why would I be jealous of her sleeping with another man? I didn't care."

He banged his head against the wall he leaned against. "But she had to rub it in my face and flirt with him right in front of me. She wanted to make me jealous. I didn't mean to kill her. I just wanted her to shut up."

His eyes locked on Alex's. "Who knew her neck would snap that easily?"

Alex stood up. "And Emerald?"

"I told you. I didn't kill her.

"I need ice and a whisky." Alex rubbed his chin, dark with stubble and the beginning of a bruise. He looked at his watch. "The closest bar open is the one in the Disco. Will you come with me?"

Olivia looked down at her youth staff uniform. "I'm not exactly dressed to go out."

Alex swiped his key card on his cabin door. "Hold on." He held up a tuxedo jacket. "It's too small for me now."

He slipped it on over her shirt. He held her out at arm's length. "It looks pretty good on you, though."

Alex took her hand and led her through the dancers to the bar in the back corner. He ordered their drinks and sat back on the barstool. He pivoted towards Olivia and leaned forward, resting his head on her shoulder. “What a night.”

Olivia reached up and rubbed his back.

Alex took a deep breath. He sat up, the flashing lights of the Disco reflecting off of his face.

The bartender threw down a couple of coasters with the ship’s logo on them and plopped their drinks down. Alex handed him his card. He scanned it and handed it back to him.

Alex picked up his glass and swirled the drink around. He breathed in the whisky's scent and then drank it down.

Alex gasped and shook his head. He signaled to the bartender for another.

He said something to Olivia.

She shook her head and cupped her ear. “I can’t hear you over the music.”

He leaned forward and spoke into her ear. “I’d forgotten how loud it is in here. Finish your drink and we’ll get out of here.” His breath was hot on her neck.

She shivered, goosebumps raced down her arms.

“You never told me where you found that picture of Nell.”

Olivia leaned back and scrunched up her face. “You aren’t going to like it.”

“Why am I not going to like it?”

“Well…”

A commotion broke out on the dance floor. A passenger who had had one too many shoved another. Barrett cut through the crowd, his head inches above the dancers. He reached the fighting parties and held them apart with his long arms.

The drunk dancer lunged at Barrett. He grabbed him by the arm and then the other passenger punched the first passenger.

"Oh, for..." Alex closed his eyes. He lifted Olivia's hair away and spoke into her ear. "I'll be back."

He crossed the dance floor and helped Barrett wrestle the passengers apart. He signaled to the DJ to cut the music and turn on the lights.

The remaining dancers groaned but slowly made their way out of the Disco.

Barrett and Alex got the passengers under control and sent them off to bed.

Alex came back and settled on the barstool next to Olivia. "What a night, huh?"

Olivia nodded and finished off her wine.

Barrett walked up behind the bar and reached a hand out to shake Alex's. "Thanks for your help, sir."

"Of course."

Olivia put down her glass. "Does that happen a lot?"

Barrett shrugged. "Enough. Especially on the first nights and the last nights of the cruise."

"Not the best way to start or end their cruise." Olivia shook her head.

Barrett laughed. "Everyone wants to get in as much fun as they can. Of course, it isn't always passengers who have too much fun. Last cruise, a crew member passed out in the women's bathroom by the pool. Nell came and got me to help her get the lady into a wheelchair so she could help her down to the Infirmary."

Olivia froze. "Nell?"

"Yeah." Barrett held his hand up below his shoulder. "Tiny little thing. She couldn't lift her by herself."

"What did the lady look like?"

Barrett described Emerald.

"She was passed out?"

"Yep. Passed out cold. Nell said she'd had one cocktail too many. It happens. Nell said the woman was upset because she'd found out that her boyfriend was married and that his wife back home was pregnant. I guess she'd gotten in a fight with her roommate who had told her he was bad news." He shrugged.

"She was like picking up dead weight. Didn't come to at all when I picked her up."

Olivia swallowed and looked at Alex. "This was in the bathroom by the pool?"

"Yeah. The out-of-order one." Barrett tilted his head and his brow furrowed. "The door was locked. Nell used a key card to open it. I guess she didn't want a passenger to find her. Not a good look for the ship to have a crew member passed out on the bathroom floor."

Alex rubbed his temple. "Did the woman have any cuts or bruises?"

Barrett nodded. "She had a cut on her forehead, but it wasn't bleeding. I figured Dr. Kohli would bandage it up when Nell took her to the Infirmary."

Alex's eyes darted toward Olivia's and he raised his eyebrow, "Did you help Nell take the crew member to the Infirmary?"

"Nah. Nell said she was going to wheel her down. Once she got my help lifting her, she didn't need any more help.
" Barrett closed his eyes and thought. "She didn't go down the elevator that goes to the Infirmary, though."

"Where did she go?"

Barrett looked up, trying to remember. "I think she headed back towards the mini golf- I think. I didn't know there was an elevator over there?"

Alex shook his head. "I don't think she was taking her to the Infirmary."

Olivia remembered Jimmy's golf ball flying over the side of the ship
and landing in the water below. She

shivered, the hairs on the back of her neck stood on end.

"Another all-nighter."

The horizon stretched out before her, the deep blue sky slowly giving way to the brilliant palette of pinks and oranges of the morning sky. The sea below seemed to shimmer and sparkle as the light slowly crept across the horizon, illuminating the vast ocean below.

Alex turned away from the sunrise and watched the pink glow wash over Olivia's face. "We need to make it a point to spend more sunrises and sunsets out on deck together."

"If I'm still here."

"Tristan hasn't told you if your contract has been renewed yet?"

Olivia shook her head. "Maybe they have another magic act scheduled already."

Alex took her hand in his and squeezed it. "I'm sure your contract will get renewed. But if it doesn't, maybe you could stay on as my guest."

Olivia looked down at Alex's hand covering hers. "You would want that? Doesn't it seem like that would be jumping the gun a little?"

Alex's fingers traced the outline of her chin. He lifted her chin up and looked in her eyes. He shook his head. "Your eyes are the same blue as the sky right after the sunrise."

"You didn't answer me."

"Olivia Grace Morgan, I can't think about anything but you. I can't imagine being here without you. And Chico."

A smile washed across Olivia's face. "He likes you, too."

"I'm glad he likes me. But what about you?"

"Very much." Olivia swallowed. "I..."

Alex cupped her face with his hands and kissed her gently on the lips.

When the kiss ended, Olivia smiled and looked into Alex's eyes, and felt an overwhelming sense of happiness.

The sun continued to rise and its golden light spread across the horizon.

The hum of the ship's engine lowered as the ship slowed. The pilot boat raced out from the harbor. They watched it pull up next to the ship. The pilot climbed on the bow of the pilot boat and leapt into the opening of their ship.

Olivia pulled the phone away from her ear and looked at it. She held it back to her ear. "You did what, Mom?"

Olivia listened to her mom's excited chatter about her trip.

"Jerry drove you all the way back to New York in that old car?" Olivia's eyes bugged out as she listened to her mom. "Oh, not straight through? You stopped in Virginia to pick up his dog? Sure. That makes it so much better."

Olivia shook her head. “I know you had a lot of luggage... Yes, the overage fees would have been high.”

Olivia rolled her eyes. “I’m glad you’re having fun. Look, I still haven’t heard if my contract is going to be renewed or not. If it isn’t, I might come home for a while.”

There was a long pause on the other end of the phone before her mother replied.

Olivia’s stomach dropped. “Don’t you want me to come home?”

Jimmy’s mom led him out of the terminal. He spotted Olivia and darted away from his mother towards her.

“Look, Mom. I have to go. I’ll call you next week and let you know what I’m doing, okay?” Olivia hung up the phone just as Jimmy reached her.

He grabbed her legs and hugged them.

Olivia peeled his arms off of her and knelt down. She pulled him in her arms and hugged him tightly. “I hope you had a fun cruise.”

“It was the best.” He pulled back, made a silly face, and raced across the sidewalk to his mom.

Tristan walked over. “Looks like you were a hit with the kiddos.”

“Jimmy and I started out a little rough, but I grew pretty fond of the little guy. I’m going to miss him.”

“Want to work as a youth counselor again this cruise?” Tristan asked.

“Oh, no. No, thank you.” Olivia shook her head. “I enjoyed it more than I thought I would, but I think I’ll stick to my magic show.”

Tristan's head shot back as he barked out a laugh. "Don't worry. I was just taking the mickey out of you! We have a new youth counselor arriving in about fifteen minutes."

"Thank goodness!" Olivia's hand shot to her chest. "You better not joke like that with Hayley. She'd walk off the ship before you could tell her it was a joke and you'd never see her again."

"Aw, she didn't hate working with the kids that much, did she?"

"She wasn't thrilled."

Tristan's face fell. "She has seemed miffed lately."

Olivia didn't know what to say to him. "Any chance you've heard anything about my contract and if it is going to be renewed?"

"Sorry. Not yet. I have a call in with Gayle, the entertainment director at half-past two. I should know something then."

Olivia bit her lip. "Thanks."

"You know I'd love to have you stay on. I think you and Hayley do a smashing job."

Olivia sighed. "That means a lot. Thanks."

Tristan's gaze followed a van as it pulled up, and a young woman stepped out. She looked around the terminal as if she was expecting someone. "Looks like your relief has arrived. The new youth counselor. I'm off to greet her."

A police car pulled up behind the van. Olivia glanced back at the crew gangway. Alex and Victor led a handcuffed Christopher off the ship and handed him off to the police. Alex turned back towards the ship. His face lit up as he recognized Olivia standing off to the side. He murmured something to Victor and then headed towards her, smiling.

"Hey."

Olivia grinned at him. "Hey, yourself."

They watched the police car pull away from the terminal and drive out of the port.

"Good riddance." Olivia's nose wrinkled.

"So. Tell me about these guys that hit on you 'all the time.' Maybe I can arrange a ride for them in a police car, too."

"You don't have anything to worry about."

Visit

https://www.amazon.com/dp/B0B5LPGSPT to see the complete series.

Visit

https://WendyNeugent.com/free-book

to get the e-book of Chico's Adoption story for free!

Gotcha!

When Olivia walked into the pet store to buy dog food for her mother's chihuahua, she wasn't looking to adopt a pet.

After all, traveling the world as an entertainer on a cruise ship isn't exactly pet friendly.

But she desperately wants to save the bird from the nasty pet shop owner.

Not only is the pet shop owner mean to the little parrot, but Olivia suspects that he is up to no good.

Can she save the parrot and take down the pet store owner, or will the pet shop owner take Olivia out?

Get this mystery ebook for free and find out!

Wendy Neugent spent close to a decade as part of an award-winning magic act performing on cruise ships all over the world. She traveled from Alaska to Venezuela, Bermuda to Tahiti, and many exotic ports of call in between.

Now, Wendy uses her insider knowledge of cruise ship life to write fun and entertaining cozy mystery books set on cruise ships.

Wendy's Cruise Ship Mysteries are the perfect books to read while taking a cruise or when you wish you were on a cruise.

Made in the USA
Middletown, DE
29 November 2024